Lorraine Hall is a part-time b̶ ̶ ̶ ̶ writer. She was born w̶ ̶ ̶ in the clouds, which, i̶ ̶ combination to spend ̶ ̶ alpha heroes and the fie̶ ̶ ̶ ̶ ̶ ̶ ̶ ̶ ̶ ̶ ̶ ̶ ̶ ̶es who win their hearts. Sh̶ ̶ ̶ ̶ ̶ ̶ ̶ ̶entially haunted house with her s̶ ̶ ̶ ̶ ate and rambunctious band of hermits-in-training. When she's not writing romance, she's reading it.

Books by Lorraine Hall

Harlequin Presents

The Prince's Royal Wedding Demand
A Son Hidden from the Sicilian
The Forbidden Princess He Craves
Playing the Sicilian's Game of Revenge
A Diamond for His Defiant Cinderella

Secrets of the Kalyva Crown

Hired for His Royal Revenge
Pregnant at the Palace Altar

The Diamond Club

Italian's Stolen Wife

Visit the Author Profile page
at Harlequin.com.

For sisters.

CHAPTER ONE

CRISTHIAN STERLING KNEW exactly where he could go and not be recognized. It got easier the older he got, the less he resembled a bewildered, hurting boy who'd just lost his parents—their terrible car accident splashed next to his picture on every paper, magazine, tabloid and so on.

The upper crust set still knew him by sight more often than not, so he preferred to celebrate his successes in more...*middle-class* establishments. Where, typically, no one would realize who he was or that his mother had been a princess and his father had been Hollywood royalty.

Inadvertently, they had both inspired his choice of profession—though their incredible wealth and prestige had passed to him and he didn't *need* to work. His mother had never known quite what to do with her fame, the public's ruthless interest in everything that made up her relationship to his father.

Though he'd only been ten when they'd died, he remembered conversations of "running away." Of disappearing, never to be found.

But his father had continued to make movies, though he'd always put Cristhian and his mother first. His mother, no matter how it had weighed on her, had continued to fulfill her royal duties to her home country of Hisla, even as she'd raised him in a modest home outside the castle walls when they weren't traveling with his father or visiting his American grandparents.

When they'd finally had enough of the paparazzi, of the way his mother's family had constantly been looking for any opportunity to drive his parents apart, they hadn't stood up for themselves. They hadn't taken control of the situation and made it right.

They'd begun to plan their escape from the bright lights of stardom.

And in the process, they'd been involved in a disastrous car crash that had killed them both instantly.

Leaving him behind.

Perhaps if he'd been allowed to stay with his father's parents in America where he'd been staying while his parents tried to find somewhere safe to escape to, he would feel differently about the whole situation these days. But instead he'd been ripped away, into his mother's royal family who didn't want him, but couldn't bear the stories of him being raised by *Americans*.

Cristhian had learned something from that. He was still working what exactly out these twenty-some years later. When his profession—one he'd carved out for himself—involved him being a finder of sorts. Runaways of the royal set, errant wives, those who wished to disappear. He found them, for whomever wanted to pay his exorbitant fee.

Some people called it mercenary. Usually the people he found who weren't happy to be escorted back to what they'd run away from.

But he knew what else awaited them out in that cold, cruel world. When you stepped out of the rules that governed your life, yourself, disaster awaited. There was only one way to deal with the unfairness of the world—it was to face all problems head-on. Running away never amounted to anything but pain. Because these royal types never stopped, never gave up. You had to beat them at their own game or lose.

So Cristhian had built himself a very clear life with very set rules. He'd stood up to the royal family who wanted to control him, and he didn't worry himself with the opinions of others.

Ever.

He studied the drink in front of him, wondered what had made his brain take a trip down *that* memory lane when he should be enjoying a good drink, perhaps a beautiful woman, in celebration of his latest runaway return.

The girl had been *thirteen*. She might not love her life in her tiny kingdom, but thirteen wasn't the age for a countess to try to make a life out there on her own. She would never thank him for his service, but she would not end up dead. He did not need any thanks. He had the satisfaction of a job well done.

He glanced around the bar. There were a lot of corporate types this Friday night. Ties loosened, top buttons undone, blazers discarded. Loud laughter and couples with surreptitious gazes around the bar like they knew they shouldn't be sitting *that* close to their coworker. Portuguese, Spanish and smatterings of English echoed across the large room.

The door opened, letting in a little gust of air, slightly cooler than the over-warm atmosphere in the bar. Cristhian sipped his drink and watched a woman hesitate in the doorway.

She was clearly alone, and for a moment he saw a flash of fear in her expression, in that hesitation. Then the woman seemed to metaphorically straighten her shoulders, push all that fear away with determination to do whatever she came to do. For a moment, he saw a flash of his mother, doing the exact same before facing a royal event.

But he forgot all about his long-lost mother when the woman smiled. Excitement sparkled in her improbably blue eyes. Her short reddish hair swung with her confident strides against her jawbone as she sauntered fully inside. She wore a boxy sort of black dress that didn't show off much of her figure, but it ended mid-thigh and showcased long, mouthwatering legs.

She didn't meet his gaze. She was on a mission, it seemed, heading straight for the bar where he sat. But her gaze was on the bartender.

She leaned forward but didn't say anything at first. The bartender sighed. "What can I get you?"

"Do you have a menu?" She had an interesting accent. Cristhian knew he'd heard it before, but it would take some thought to remind himself what tiny European country it belonged to. Something far north of southern Portugal where they were currently.

The bartender scoffed with an eye roll.

"Allow me to make a suggestion," Cristhian offered, earning the woman's curious gaze. He was half convinced she was wearing some kind of color-correcting contacts. The shade of blue didn't suit her at all.

And yet she was beautiful. Delicate shoulders and a

determined demeanor. A cupid's-bow mouth and expressive eyebrows that she arched at him now. As if to say *go on, and you had better impress me*.

Cristhian grinned. He *was* impressive in pretty much all things. He didn't consider this conceit so much as a healthy appreciation of facts. "Beirão," he said, turning his attention to the bartender. "Put it on my tab."

The bartender nodded and turned to put the woman's drink together. Cristhian gestured to the empty seat next to him. "Join me."

She narrowed her eyes a little at him. "Typically, that sort of invitation is offered as a *request*, sir."

He didn't so much as flinch. Didn't hide his interest. Why bother? "I'm not typical. *Naturalmente*."

She laughed. A lyrical sound that was tinged with a little huskiness that intrigued him more than he could remember being intrigued for quite some time. With an elegance that spoke of training—royal training at that—she slid onto the stool next to him.

The hint of royal had him studying her more closely. Her clothes, the haircut, these things were all firmly *not* royal. But Cristhian knew well that facades could be deceiving.

In a corporate bar in Faro? He was letting his work get to him.

The bartender slid her the drink he'd ordered for her, and a refill of Cristhian's own drink. The woman took a tentative sip, and he watched her reaction intently.

"Perfect," she said, then flashed him a dazzling smile. The kind of smile that spelled trouble.

Luckily, Cristhian excelled at trouble. Wrangling it into all the rules he liked to follow.

"So, what brings you to Faro?"

"Work," she said without hesitation. And royals didn't work, he reminded himself. "But I'm done now and headed home tomorrow."

"And where's home?"

This she hesitated over. Which could be chalked up to a woman being careful of what she told a man. "Hamburg," she eventually offered. "For now."

The accent wasn't a perfect match, but the *for now* made him think she wasn't a German native. It all added up, and he was celebrating a job well done, not *working*, so he needed to relax.

Enjoy.

"Are you local?" she asked him, continuing to sip at her drink. Real diamonds winked at her ears. Expensive diamonds.

He tried not to frown at himself. No more work. *Celebrate.* "I'm more of a nomad myself. Though I find myself in Faro often enough."

"A nomad," she said, as if considering. "No home base, then?"

"I have many home bases."

She angled her chin at him, just so. Haughty, but not in a standoffish kind of way. It suited her, this unearned confidence. "With a woman at each?"

His mouth quirked. "Ah, you impinge my character."

She made a waving gesture. "And you don't deny it."

"There is no specific woman in any such home base. I find relationships don't really fit in with my schedule of travel. My work takes up most of my life."

Something about the word *work* had her expression

tightening. Some of that easy bemusement melting out of her eyes.

"You look like someone with a home fire burning," he said, hoping to get some of that sparkle back in her gaze.

She shook her head, no amusement. A hint of sadness at the edge of her features instead. "Not the way you mean. But responsibilities, I suppose. *Work*. Calling me home." She took a deep drink, set the glass on the bar. "But not until tomorrow," she said forcefully, staring hard at the bar. "For tonight, I'll enjoy freedom from responsibilities."

"Well, I suppose it's kismet then. I, too, am enjoying my freedom tonight. Freedom is much more fun with some company, don't you think?"

She studied him, some of that amusement returning to her expression. "I do," she agreed. "Is there anywhere around here with dancing?"

"There's a club right across the street. Rua Noturna." He nodded to the door.

She slid off her stool. "Let's go then."

Zia Rendall had not intended to pick up a man this evening. It wasn't fully out of the scope of her plans. She might have *hoped* she'd meet someone who made her insides hum just from a look, but she'd known how unlikely that would be.

Her week of freedom had been hard-won to say the least. It hadn't just been escaping the palace and Lille— she'd spent most of her adolescence perfecting those things. It had been about getting out *and* flying under the radar for a week.

Luckily her twin sister, Beaugonia, was an expert at

so many things, she'd helped. Procured the colored contacts Zia now wore, the dye she'd used in her hair once she'd been free of the palace. Beau had even done the honors and chopped off Zia's hair.

It was Beau's expertise at computers that had gotten Zia fake identification, a flight to Portugal, and a hotel first in Lisbon, then the past few days in Faro.

Zia had left a note for her parents and a promise to return, and Zia knew that and Beau's efforts to smooth over their parents' anger would be the only reasons they wouldn't send armed guards after her.

Not that they hadn't tried, no doubt, but more on the down-low. They would go harder once her week was up. Tomorrow, bright and early, she had to be on a plane back to Lille or things would…implode, no doubt.

So this was it. She hadn't been about to throw herself at just *any* man for the sake of it. Her fun had included being a normal human, walking about without guards. Sleeping, eating, drinking and doing whatever she fancied, rather than follow royal protocol and a schedule someone else had made for her.

It had been like breathing for the first time. She had lived for herself. While she was still worried about Beau at home alone with their parents, she hadn't had to think of how to protect her with every step. For the first time in her life, a weight she'd grown so accustomed to she had stopped noticing it had lifted.

And now it was all over. Back to the palace. Back to the responsibilities she did not want but had to face. For Beau.

Except it wasn't over just yet. She still had tonight.

Walking into that bar and meeting the gaze of *this*

man had made it very easy to determine that a wildly handsome stranger, and maybe even a night with him, would be the cherry on top of her last night of freedom.

She had lied to him about some things, but not about freedom and this being her last day of it. Tomorrow she'd return to Lille, her role as Princess Zia Asta Alberte Elisabeth Rendall and the responsibilities waiting for her.

Like a royal wedding in the spring. Crown Prince Lyon Traverso was handsome enough, and not *mean*, by any stretch. But he was aloof, at best. And had plans for his kingdom that he wanted no help with. She would have no say as his wife. Her role would essentially be to pop out princes and princesses until the kingdom was satisfied.

She had no desire to be a broodmare for anyone, let alone a virtual stranger, but it had certainly not been her choice, this political merger her father had planned and inked out. Heir or no, she had no say in her father's choices. She was promised to Lyon.

She could have refused, she supposed, but her parents had made it clear if she did not meet her responsibilities, everyone would pay the price. Mostly her twin, who was…*eccentric*.

At least, that's what the palace called it.

This week was the closest thing she was ever going to have to making her own choices, and as much as she hated that, she hated the idea of Beau suffering the slings and arrows of their father more.

Zia didn't want to think about any of it tonight. She wanted to feel freedom in this last night of it. She wanted to drink, to dance.

She wanted the stranger she'd picked up at a bar. Sinfully handsome, too charming for anyone's good. He was impossibly tall, with broad shoulders to match. Dark hair cropped short, dark eyes, wearing all black like some kind of evil spirit. His smile was sin itself. He was no doubt the type to love and leave.

So, perfect. Maybe an evil spirit, but one who would be a lot of fun before she had to spend the rest of her life metaphorically chained to a monarchy and a man she didn't care about in the least.

But she cared about her sister, and—

She wasn't thinking about that tonight. She was thinking about the man dancing with her. His body was a hard wall of heat. His hand on her back felt like a brand, but it was nothing to the way they moved together. Like two interlocking parts.

While lights flashed and music thrummed around them, it felt like they were the only two people in existence. Which was a freedom even greater and more exhilarating than the one she'd found on her own. Because she was still a princess when it was just her. When she was with *him,* she was a nameless woman. Nothing about her title mattered. Nothing about her country or the expectations laid upon her or who she needed to protect. She could just be whoever she was underneath that.

She'd begun to be afraid there was nothing. But this man laughed when she told a joke. He listened when she explained what she liked about Portugal. There was a give-and-take to their conversation, to their dancing. Not just *control.*

In fact, it seemed as if there was no control between either of them at all. Everything that existed here was elemental. Nothing but chemistry and heat and want.

His hand skimmed down her spine, inciting a jolt of desire, a deep, dark craving swirling around inside her, and an arrow of heat straight to her core. She pressed herself even more firmly to him, and his leg skimmed between hers, making the faintest contact with her bare inner thigh.

Her breath came out in a huff she should have done a better job of hiding. Especially when his chuckle was low and rumbled along her exposed neck. She suddenly understood those over-the-top vampire romances her sister loved to read. She'd do anything to feel his mouth on her neck, no matter how reckless or ill-advised.

So she followed all that reckless down the rabbit hole and lifted to her toes to press her mouth to his, here in this crowded club, where she was no one, except a woman who wanted him.

He tasted like danger. It shot through her bloodstream. Stronger than any drink she'd had tonight. Heat and need and the whirling, sparkling joy of doing whatever the hell she wanted.

Royal protocol be damned. *Finally*.

"I have a hotel suite not far from here." His voice was a rasp in her ear. "And a car to get us there."

It was all the invitation she needed. "Let's go."

CHAPTER TWO

CRISTHIAN DID NOT consider himself particularly uptight, despite a life well organized to suit his needs. He enjoyed women, wherever and whenever the opportunity presented itself. He was not choosy.

But he was usually careful. There were ground rules set. *He* was in control, so that nothing messy came from such an encounter. He ordered his life just how he liked it—whether that be business or pleasure. This had always been…easy.

This woman had blasted rules and control all to hell. He had driven too fast, breaking too many laws, with one hand curled in her hair. While her mouth had been pressed in impressively imaginative ways against his neck.

He could not remember a more desperate stumble into any of the many apartments and homes he owned, no needy rush to a hotel room in his many travels. He could not recall a time when the only possible thought in his head was to explore every last inch of her naked body, over and over again. Not since he'd been a teen eager for that first taste of something he only barely understood had he ever felt so out of control.

Control, that tenet to his life, but she seemed too pretty

a flame to try to tame. She was brave and impetuous, but with something more careful underneath. Something that spoke to him, as if it needed tending. He had no desire to structure her in some way to suit his needs. He'd rather just…experience something. Without those rules and lines he knew kept him safe.

There was something revelatory in a lack of safety, of control. And the way the minute they stepped inside his hotel suite, she wrapped around him like the tide, pulling him under, into wave after wave until he was drowning in her. Her short hair was silk in his fisted hand, her mouth a fire of need against his.

He pressed her against the door he'd just closed. Unwinding her arms from his neck so he could pull the dress up and off of her.

Her eyes met his, that blue that didn't fit at all. And yet they were still part of that ocean pulling him under. That and the slender, athletic body underneath. Not his usual type, and yet his mouth watered.

Her underthings were silk, terribly expensive, and any alarm bells that rang in the back of his head that she might be more than he bargained for, that she might know who he was despite the fact that they hadn't exchanged names, were completely muffled by the sound she made when he pressed his hand between her legs.

He took his time exploring the contours of her body while she shivered and begged. He slid the straps of her bra down, following the slope of her shoulder with his mouth. She unbuttoned his shirt, pushed it off him.

It was like a battle. Fencing, maybe. Move and countermove. His mouth on her breast. Her hands on his zipper. Her mouth hot, needy, demanding. And yet she submitted to every demand of his own.

She tasted like some brand-new delicacy, felt like some hidden garden that grew things he'd never seen before. He didn't recognize himself or the strange sensations ricocheting inside him as he devoured her mouth with tongue and teeth.

Her hand fisted over him, gave one slow stroke. "Now," she panted, meeting his gaze. It was an order, and yet… "Please," she added breathlessly.

There was nothing else beyond that *please*. Not a second's thought. Only a need so all-encompassing he'd later wonder if he'd suffered some sort of medical event that had rendered him completely brain-dead.

He lifted her and with quick strides had her laid out on the large, luxurious bed. He rid himself of the rest of his clothes in seconds flat, moved over her, slid home with a pounding desire that blotted everything else out except the slow, slick slide of perfection.

She exploded around him in a rush, so hot and fast it nearly took him out. The word *kismet* seemed to dance around them, like by uttering such a silly pickup line at that bar he had spoken it into existence.

Fate. Destiny. Her.

He didn't even know her name. But that seemed such a shallow thing in the moment. In the panting of her breath, the soft velvet of her skin. The molten give of her.

He rolled her on top of him, and she balanced herself with two hands on his chest. She grinned down at him.

She moved against him, arching that beautiful body. He slid possessive hands down her sides, then urged her to move faster. To chase these things rioting inside him.

He toyed with her nipple and her breathing hitched, the graceful pace she'd set fractured.

Into something wild. Frenzied. There was only the sounds of their breathing, interrupted moans and sighs, their bodies moving together in perfect rhythm. She cried out, shuddered over and over again, and still he held on to that tiniest thread of control.

He rolled her under him, slowed it down to take every ounce of pleasure out of every second. Her moan was a shot of adrenaline. That lost look on her face would stay etched into his memory, possibly forever.

When he followed her over that last edge, he couldn't help but feel like they'd both been found.

Zia had to leave. She shouldn't have stayed as long as she did. It was nearly morning. Not only did she have a plane to catch, but this man could never know who she really was. The more time she gave him, the more ammunition she gave him to figure out her secret.

Throughout the course of the evening, he'd looked at her slightly sideways, like he suspected something. But she'd only needed to kiss him, touch him to make that look disappear.

She couldn't risk more, no matter how much she wanted to.

Regret didn't coil inside her like a weight so much as a wistful kind of longing. For a different life, where she could enjoy any kind of intimate relationship without fear all her misdeeds—meant or inadvertent, true or false—could be sold to the press for so much money it would be hard to blame a person for it.

She thought maybe she could live under the weight

of the press's scrutiny, but she would not be able to live under the weight of her parents' forever disappointment. She'd already caused them too much grief. It wasn't their fault, any more than it was hers, that they were the king and queen. It was simply the happenstance of the world.

And her world meant responsibility. Because if she didn't meet it, Beaugonia would suffer. Her parents did not understand Beaugonia. They saw her lack of following their rules as defiance, some act of violence instead of just who Beau was. So true to herself she couldn't pretend. But it wasn't that simple, or Beau wouldn't suffer from the panic attacks that had their parents viewing her as something…inferior.

No, Zia wouldn't let that be Beau's fate. When she was home, her parents focused on her, on the upcoming wedding. On plans for Lille's partnership with Lyon's home country, Divio.

Then it would be Beau's turn for freedom.

So Zia eased out of the warm, soft bed, away from the large, gorgeous man, still fast asleep.

Zia was an expert at sneaking around. Her entire adolescence had been a study in it. The more guards her father had put on her, the sneakier she'd had to be.

The king would be at his wits' end today, worrying if she'd come back at all. Making plans for if she didn't. And all of those plans would be ready to be accomplished the second she broke her promise.

If she didn't make her flight, all hell would break loose.

Zia's time was up. She should be satisfied. Happy she got to do all the things she wanted.

She collected her discarded clothes, then gave *him* a

look over her shoulder. He didn't so much as stir. For a moment, she felt the strangest pang. She'd gone into this knowing it was a fling. A one-night stand, and she had no doubt he had done the same. He'd made that clear.

Maybe it had gotten a little muddled in the time in between. When he'd fed her and they'd laughed over steak sandwiches and a bottle of wine. They had not gotten into their personal lives, but they had spoken of places they'd traveled.

He was even more well-traveled than she and could weave entertaining stories of even the most boring museums. He was a fascinating man…even when she knew nothing about him.

So when they'd fallen into his bed again, it had been like they were old friends. When they'd dozed together and turned to each other all over again, she'd had the passing thought of how nice a life like this might be. Not two people fighting for control. Just a kind of… comradery. A partnership. A friendship. With amazing sex thrown in.

Muddled, yes, her feelings were, but the sex was not. It was explosive. Irresistible. An unquenchable hunger, like they were each a dessert they couldn't quite get enough of no matter how they gorged themselves.

But it was over now. There would be no going back. She would be married come spring. Maybe…maybe she could find some semblance of this with her husband, the crown prince.

But Zia doubted it.

Lyon had made it clear that, like her father, he had expectations, roles for her to fill. He was not interested in *her*. He would not ask her opinion on the music in the

club or make her a sandwich. Even meeting the prince
only twice, she knew this.

But she had also known her whole life, she was not
destined for all the *normal* and *simple* she craved. She
was a princess. The heir. Her only role was for her country.

No matter how joyous, how right this week, last night
had felt.

The future felt like a dead weight in her chest—not a
new feeling, but it felt heavier now. Because she'd seen
what could be this week. She'd thought that would give
her the relief to make it through her responsibilities.

But instead it had given her a taste of joy. Not just
him, but everything she'd done this week. To walk the
streets a nobody. To window-shop without guards, or an
assistant having to make the purchases for her. To experience all the normalcies of life, on her own, and not worry
about taking a misstep that Beau might be punished for.
Because for all she rebelled in the privacy of the castle,
she had known her parents would inflict an incredible
avalanche of pain if she did it in public.

In this week, she got to make mistakes. She got to
be whoever she wanted to be. Rude. Polite. Overzealous. Hysterical.

In absolute *lust* with a complete stranger.

Oh, she knew she was privileged, but her privilege
came with a price, and sometimes that price felt so heavy
she could scarcely breathe. And still it was the privilege,
and her sister back home, that meant she knew she had
to follow her responsibilities.

Back to Lille. To a marriage she didn't want. A prison
sentence when she wasn't sure what crime she'd ever

committed except being born the pretty twin. The elegant twin. The one with natural social graces and whose panic didn't take over at any given moment.

Careful not to sigh, she slid out of the hotel suite, put back together as best she could be. She took a taxi to the airport and flew back home.

Back to being Princess Zia Rendall.

And all the weight that went with that.

CHAPTER THREE

CRISTHIAN HADN'T STOPPED her sneak-away exit. It was best to not share any awkward goodbyes. No matter how often they'd turned into and over each other, they had not shared names. They both knew what it had been.

It had been *irregular,* the conversations they'd had in between the bouts of unbelievable pleasure, but there was no point in dwelling on that.

But dwell on it he did.

For months.

He couldn't seem to eradicate the woman whose name he didn't even know out of his mind. He could have looked for her. Sometimes the memory of one night drove him so crazy, he nearly began a search. He was a finder. It would be easy to do just that.

For *what*? One random woman? Who he knew next to nothing about except that she was well-traveled and gorgeous? That she liked music more than art, gardens more than museums. And what she sounded like when she came apart in his arms.

What was he going to do? Track her down? *Date* her?

It was so ludicrous every time he got to that part in the circular thought process of not being able to forget her, he laughed. And moved on.

For a time.

When a case finally came in, one worthy of his skills and with the kind of payment he preferred, Cristhian took the first plane out to the small country of Lille, nestled in northern Europe.

A job would surely solve this…problem of his. By the end of it, he would forget about some nameless woman and her one night in his bed over six months ago.

But when he was greeted at the airport by a royal guard to the king, Cristhian found himself all too reminded of his mystery woman, because the guard's accent was *exactly* like hers. She had called Hamburg home, but he had a feeling even if she'd been telling the truth about her current home, she was *from* this country.

He was escorted into a blacked-out car and driven to the castle. The country was small and clearly took its traditions very seriously. If not for the people walking streets in jeans and noses pressed to phones, Cristhian might have felt like he was stepping back in time. The architecture was very old, the buildings crowded together, until they reached the center of the capital where a grand square spread out in front of a modest castle. All very old stones and towers and stained glass.

It reminded him of his mother's country. The one that still tried to lure him back from time to time. For a photo op or to stir up stories that made the royal family look good. Luckily, as his mother had been the seventh child of his grandparents, and his aunts and uncles all had multiple children, Cristhian had only a small title, and a few holdings he had negotiated when he had stood up to his aunt, the current queen, and demanded release on his twenty-first birthday.

He had refused to run away. He had fought instead. And maybe he wasn't as perfectly free of their titles and their legacies as he'd like, but he was *free*.

Somehow, even now, worse than thoughts of those people, were thoughts of the woman he was supposed to forget.

He could picture her here. Walking the street to whatever job she had. Shoulders back, that athletic body carefully hidden away in something boxy. Maybe she was some kind of athlete. *That* would be interesting.

And neither here nor there. Because that had been a nameless night. He would not look for her here. There was no point. He had a job to do.

But if *kismet* stepped in…

The car pulled to a stop in the back of the castle, and Cristhian was led inside, through curving hallways and up elaborate staircases. He was asked to wait in an interior room, and he seated himself on a plush chair, taking in the surroundings. Old, well-preserved wallpaper in deep blues. Dark wood polished to a shine. He vaguely remembered a visit here as a child. Most of the royal visits of his childhood sort of ran together, but this one he remembered because his father was supposed to have been filming somewhere, but he'd left the set to accompany Mother, knowing she hated taking on these royal appearances alone.

She'd been so happy at his surprise arrival. Sometimes Cristhian thought that was the best memory he had of the two of them, when there were so many. But his father's important gesture, and his mother's heartfelt gratitude, had stuck with him in perfect imagery.

It was strange to realize that the memory did not make

him as sad as it once had. There was a strange contentment mixed in with the grief. Perhaps their lives had been cut too short, and perhaps they'd had a part in the mistakes that had led them here, but they'd had each other. A love so bright and encompassing they'd both sacrificed for it.

But they'd never sacrificed him, and as Cristhian had navigated the world as an adolescent in high-end circles, he'd realized how very rare that was, and how mixed in all the tragedy he had a little bit of luck on his side.

But none of that was why he was here, so he studied the rest of the room and put the past away.

There was a large royal portrait dominating one wall. Cristhian recognized the current king, and his queen standing next to him. The young girls must be their twin daughters.

Cristhian frowned at the painting. The girls couldn't have been more than ten or so in it, so it was an old painting. But something about them…felt familiar.

An uncomfortable foreboding moved through him, but he didn't have time to analyze it as the king walked in.

Cristhian got to his feet and took the king's outstretched hand. He knew the royal protocol in different countries as he no doubt would if his mother had lived into his adolescence. He considered it a part of his job, but for a strange out-of-body moment he wondered if he'd learned all these silly rules for *her*, because it would have made her proud.

He gave a short bow with the handshake. "King Rendall."

"Cristhian. I haven't seen you since you were a boy."

The man slapped him on the shoulder, then gestured to the chair he'd been sitting in.

Cristhian fortified himself for the inevitable comment about his mother. How beautiful she was, how kind, how she was missed. He settled back into the chair knowing all these things were true, but when strangers commented on her he felt a wave of fury that no one had *helped* her. That she had suffered under all these people who had seen her as a perfect, untouchable princess.

When she'd just been a woman. His mother.

He forced a smile and tried to ignore the ghost that haunted him so often in these royal meetings.

But King Rendall said nothing else about his mother. He handed Cristhian a leather binder with the royal seal of Lille on it. "I have it on good authority you not only help, Cristhian, but you keep secrets."

"All my work is confidential, Your Majesty."

"I am depending on it. This is of the utmost importance to me. None of my own men could accomplish what I need these past few months. We have used every last resource we could. You're my last hope with the most important thing in the world to me."

Cristhian opened the folder and was met with a slick trickle of ice down his spine.

"The princess has run away," King Rendall explained. "It has been months now. Her sister assures us she is alive and well, but she has no other information. I need her found. I need her back."

The princess.

She didn't look the same in this picture. Her hair was a deep, dark brown in this royal portrait. Long and around her shoulders. Her eyes were a mesmerizing green that matched her hair and fair skin. But he would recognize that mouth, the quirk of a smirk underneath that royal smile, anywhere.

Princess Zia Rendall was his mystery woman.

And now he had to track her down.

Zia shivered as she tended the cookstove fire. Outside, polar night was just beginning to lift. It was midafternoon, and the sky was an interesting shade of blue. Her life here on this tiny polar island was always *interesting*.

But it was coming to an end. Not because she wanted it to. She quite enjoyed the cold, the isolation, the stark beauty of it all. But an island like this did not have the facilities for a woman to give birth. So, as she approached her seventh month of pregnancy, she would have to leave.

Maybe she would come back. Maybe she wouldn't. Everything would depend on how well she kept up her new identity throughout the birthing process.

Zia rubbed an absent hand over her belly. She had expected to be *terrified* of becoming a mother. After all, it certainly wasn't planned, but with every month she found herself looking forward to it more and more. To have the space and freedom to take care of her children as she saw fit felt like a gift.

Labor, however, did terrify her. And made her wish for things she couldn't have. Like her sister at her side, or her mother simply because Mother had actually given birth and would know how to calm her down, or even…

Well, it didn't make much sense to think about the man who'd had a hand in this. She didn't know anything about him, and so she was on her own.

The best for all involved. She couldn't imagine her

parents' reaction to her pregnancy, especially if they found out the circumstances of *how* it had happened. They certainly wouldn't allow some commoner to have any part in it. No doubt she'd have to hear about hush money again, like when her father had paid a substantial sum to Leopold, the classmate she'd fancied herself in love with, and sneaked out to shed that innocence everyone had told her was so important.

In the aftermath, she wasn't so much heartbroken about Leopold. She was just heartbroken that nothing in her life could be *normal*. It all had to be palace shenanigans, even something as intimate as a young woman's first time.

So this whole pregnancy was a strange kind of freedom. Running away, for good this time. A new identity. So that the palace didn't have a say in this thing that she still couldn't qualify as a mistake.

She rubbed her hands over the paltry heat the stove gave off. She didn't allow herself to think about how the pregnancy had happened very often. She'd had to focus on the practicalities of everything, and that kept her mind busy.

First, she'd had to accept she was pregnant. Which had not come easily. She'd felt poorly for a good two months before Beau had confronted her about it. In her very pragmatic way, laptop in hand.

Zia, I have searched your symptoms and this combination seems to point toward a pregnancy.

Zia had scoffed at her sister. Then...

You did use protection with that one-night stand, didn't you? Beau had demanded, like she knew anything about sex or one-night stands.

But Zia had been forced to come to a rather startling conclusion.

Some of the time...

Beau had tsked and shaken her head and procured her a pregnancy test without anyone at the palace getting wind of it.

When Zia had seen the positive result, she hadn't had the good sense to feel chastised. For a moment, there'd been the strangest bubble of joy. Like having a connection to that man meant something and wasn't just irresponsible. Like this was her way out when there was *no* way out. Because she could hardly marry Lyon while pregnant with someone else's baby, or anyone else for that matter. An illegitimate child meant her father could not control her life in all the ways he always had.

But slowly she'd come to realize that didn't make it a *good* thing. There were consequences for imploding everyone's lives. And so, to Zia's way of thinking, the only way to deal with this new wrinkle in her life was to run away.

For good this time.

Beau, per usual, was her saving grace. She had figured out everything to allow Zia to start a new life as someone else. She had insisted she could handle the consequences of a life in the palace without Zia there to guard her or act as heir.

Zia had argued. Vehemently. With tears, but Beau had been surprisingly determined. And the only thing that had gotten Zia to let her sister take on the consequences of Zia's own actions was the fact she now had someone besides her sister to protect.

Innocent, helpless babies growing inside her. Who did *not* deserve a life in that castle, being treated like mistakes.

All Zia had had to do was escape then…and she'd proven she was an expert at that. So she'd gotten out, and with Beau's help built this little life under a fake name on a tiny polar island that had mostly been shrouded in polar night for the duration of her pregnancy.

She'd built a small little business designing online exercise programs for people who wanted to do everything at home and only talk to their trainer via email or text—another one of Beau's brilliant ideas. Zia loved it. She even loved life on the polar island, the cozy mystery of polar night. She loved the village and her introverted lifestyle.

Trips to the mainland for her monthly checkups had yielded another surprise.

Twins.

Maybe it should have concerned her. A higher-risk pregnancy, the doctor had explained. But she'd been overjoyed. Just like she'd always had Beau, her babies would always have each other.

She tried to think of things in happy terms only—she was quite positive that was better for the babies growing inside her than anxiety and fear. She refused to consider the *scary*. Like never seeing Beau again outside of a screen. Like being alone, without a partner or a friend to lean on when she needed it. Like the father of these babies never knowing they existed, and being happy that way.

No, only good thoughts were allowed. Her babies would have each other, and they would have her. Maybe she'd failed at protecting Beau, maybe she didn't know how to find the identity of their father, but she'd work so hard to not fail her children. At least not in the ways her own parents had failed her.

She'd learned something from failing Beau. She could never put herself first. That way led to pain.

Which wasn't a very happy thought either, so she focused on making herself a little lunch, ignoring the fact she had to decide where she was going to *have* those babies. Beau had given her two options where she thought she'd be safe from her identity being discovered.

She'd have to chop her hair off again and hope that and the way her body had changed with the pregnancy would throw people off.

She was still surprised news of her disappearance hadn't found any media outlet yet. There were no stories about a canceled wedding. Short missives from Beau came and assured Zia everything at the palace was fine despite it.

Since she had babies to grow, Zia allowed herself to believe that even if it was very unlikely.

Happy, happy thoughts.

Her routine and internal reverie were interrupted by a harsh knock on the door. *Odd.* She had hired someone closer to town to deliver her mail and groceries, but that was only on Tuesdays. This was Thursday.

Maybe something important had come through. *Or maybe…* Fear jostled through her, but that was ridiculous. If her father had found her, sent men to collect her, they wouldn't knock.

Zia edged toward the window next to the door, tried to look out without being seen. There was a man out there. Bundled up in all black, a stocking cap low on his head. Despite the swirling winds, he didn't look the least bit cold.

But there was something familiar in that height, in the way the man stood…in everything. Her whole body seemed to go lax as she recognized the figure on her porch.

It was *him*. Something like joy surged through her. Silly, she knew, and yet there it was. How had he found her? *Why* had he found her? She nearly smiled.

Until his gaze lifted, met hers through the glass, and offered nothing but pure icy fury.

CHAPTER FOUR

CRISTHIAN DID NOT find anger to be a productive emotion. He preferred to diffuse any boiling intensity with whatever suited the moment—a joke, withdrawal, distraction. Fury led to rash decisions as much as fear did.

And what was anger but fear with a target?

His target stood on the other side of that glass.

A *princess*. He knew the kind of games royalty played. He'd been well-versed all his life. The manipulations and maneuverings his mother had gone to great lengths to try to escape. Then, when she'd died instead, he'd been jostled about, isolated from anyone who actually cared, as though he were merely an inanimate object to be possessed or disposed of. A narrative to be protected, not a life to be protected.

Sometimes he thought he was at peace with it.

Sometimes he realized he was four even close.

He watched Zia through the window. She took a deep breath, then disappeared. Before he could find any emotion about that, the doorknob turned, and she opened it. She stood there, framed by the rustic door.

She looked so different—dark hair, green eyes. And yet the same—the slope of her nose, the point of her chin.

That regal way she held herself that he'd noted and dismissed in his sexual haze.

Except in the here and now, she seemed softer. More…

Everything inside him dropped out as his gaze lowered. He heard nothing but a high buzzing in his ears. He saw nothing now but a very rounded belly underneath a fuzzy sweater that could not hide it.

A *pregnant* belly.

"You had better come inside," she said in that voice he remembered all too well. Like she was all too used to ordering people around. "It's very cold."

He didn't feel the cold at all. Hadn't, since he'd seen her in that window. And he had no desire to step inside what seemed a cozy enough little cabin out here on this tundra. He wanted to stay rooted to this spot. Or rewind time. *Something.* But he was a man of action.

He had to be.

He stepped inside, let her close the door behind him. It was certainly warmer in here, out of the bitter wind, but he wasn't sure it was warm enough for her…condition. He stared at it now, too many things inside him jostling for space when he'd long ago learned that every feeling, thought, and action had an ordered space within.

She'd jumbled it all up almost seven months ago. Now, again. *Seven months.* "What is this?" he demanded, his voice too rough.

"Perhaps you should tell me why you're here first," she said, with a kind of businesslike demeanor that infuriated him beyond reason.

Fury is just fear with a target.

He wanted to growl at his internal monologue, but he didn't.

"Were you…looking for me?" she asked carefully. There was a neutral look on her face, but he saw something he didn't like in her eyes. A kind of hope.

For a moment, he was rendered perfectly frozen by it. *Hope.* When he had settled *hope* firmly behind him long, long ago. When he'd realized would always be the only person looking out for his own good. When he'd realized he had to take a stand against the forces who wanted him to be nothing more than an anecdote trotted out when they were trying to hide their more sordid truths.

Uncle Gregio found with his pants around his ankles in a young woman's room? Let's run an in-depth story on the poor orphaned child of a princess and an actor, raised benevolently by the grieving family—ha!—left behind. Pictures. Of him. Of his parents' crash. All of it dragged out again.

No, hope was useless, but he had learned it could be a weapon.

It felt like he'd been assaulted. A child. A *child* growing inside this beautiful woman. A *royal* child.

Still, he needed a weapon to fight all this. So he could lie. Get under all her defenses and get all the information he desired in seconds flat with said lie, no doubt. Let her believe in that hope until he'd gotten every answer he needed to know how to move forward, and then do whatever needed to be done to fix…this.

But he'd made promises to himself long ago about what kind of man he wanted to be. What kind of legacy he would leave his parents' memories.

And since he was the only one he trusted to make that legacy, he gave Zia the truth.

"My name is Cristhian Sterling. I was hired by your

father to track you down. When he gave me the details of
your disappearance early this week, I saw a photograph
and this is when I recognized you. He did not mention…"
Cristhian waved a hand at her stomach.

"My father's men have been looking for me for months.
He hired you *this week*?"

"I am a finder, Zia. I would have found you months
ago if he'd come to me."

Something about the word *finder* must have struck
her, because she tilted her head and studied him. "Cristhian Sterling. I know that name." Her eyebrows drew
together as though she were thinking.

There was some strange relief in her having not known
who he was either those months ago. That, if nothing
else, the night they had shared had been honest. True.

But a tense, coiling dread at the idea she *knew* anything about him now that she knew his identity wiped
away any relief.

"You…you tracked down Lady Lina Sorenson," she
said after a while. "A friend of mine. Years ago. We
were fourteen."

He immediately remembered the name, because it
had been one of the first cases he'd taken on as an official job, on his own, after helping a few of his mother's
relatives track down people.

"You saved her, actually," Zia continued. "She was in
quite a dire situation."

Cristhian shrugged, remembering all too well how
close the young teen had been to being left to the whims
of a group of very dangerous gentleman. "This is my
job."

Zia inclined a royal nod. "Ah, yes. So you are here

to drag me back to my father." She shook her head. "He doesn't know." She rested her hands over her stomach as if to protect the life inside it. She kept her gaze calm and on his. "It's best if he doesn't."

"Does the father know?" he asked, once again gesturing toward her belly. And maybe he knew what her answer would be. Maybe he knew all too well what he'd just walked into.

But he wanted her to say it. In no uncertain terms.

"Cristhian." Her voice was scolding, slightly disdainful. "*You* are the father."

And that complicated *everything*.

Zia still couldn't quite believe this was happening. A name for the man she'd spent the past six months dreaming about. What had brought him here. *Her father*. His job. She knew *of* him, even if she didn't know him, and that she hadn't expected at all.

And still, she found herself wanting to throw her arms around him. He was *here*, and it felt as if…it meant something. Because now he could know, and didn't that change everything?

But she could tell from the look on his face that it meant and changed *nothing*.

"So, you were never planning on telling me," he said, a harsh statement. An indictment, not a question.

She blinked at him. He had been there and knew just how little they knew of each other, so the indictment felt patently unfair. "I did not even know your *name*, where you came from. How was I supposed to tell you?" Of course, he'd found her, but that had been with her father's help. It had been by *accident*.

"You have ample resources, Zia." Her name rolled off his tongue, and in his unique, piecemeal accent of too many different places to count, her whole body lit up in reaction.

She could not allow that to distract her from the important thing here. Protecting her children. Protecting *herself*. Her father had sent him, and she did not consider her father an evil man, exactly.

She just knew that what was best for the kingdom was his only priority, and nothing else ranked against that. Not her well-being, not Beau's. Not their mother's. The kingdom and only the kingdom. She couldn't even blame him for that—he'd been bred from the cradle to think and feel and act that way.

She did not know why she couldn't have absorbed his blind faith in the crown above all else, but she had not been able to. Perhaps only men could be that foolish.

And now this man was here, father of her children or not, as an arm of that crown. And she could not forget that. The crown had never cared about *her*. Only what she kind of tool she could be used as.

"The hotel would have had my name," Cristhian continued. "Someone at the bar, the dancing club. So many avenues would have led you to my name and *me* if you had only tried."

She supposed all of that was true, but it never would have occurred to her, which felt like an insult to her intelligence, she supposed. Or maybe how sheltered she was, no matter how hard she tried to be otherwise. But there was no point in lying, in trying to save face.

If her father had hired him, he knew every unsavory detail of her already.

"None of that ever occurred to me, Cristhian. *I* am not a finder of lost things. I am simply a princess. Not even that anymore. I have left that life behind."

"Unfortunately, you are wrong. You are just another runaway princess who would do best if she were returned to the responsible people in her life. We will leave at once."

She sighed heavily. It had been much nicer when he'd only been a fantasy. When she could make him into the man she wanted. Now he'd ruined it, by being like every other man in her acquaintance. Sure he—or the king who'd supplied him the information—knew everything.

When Cristhian clearly knew nothing. He was being paid by the king. And he hadn't taken this new piece of information into consideration. Because his involvement in her pregnancy changed everything.

"Do you honestly think you can return me to the palace like *this* and escape unscathed? I can only imagine what my father will do now. You're not a commoner, are you? Your mother was…some kind of royalty in her own right, was she not?"

He did not respond immediately to that. Instead looked fully impassive, so she cast back trying to remember the story of him. The finder of royal pedigree. His father had been American. A movie star? Something like that. But his mother… "They call you a prince."

"I am *not* a prince."

"Your mother was a princess." She didn't remember all the details, but after Lina's return, there was much talk about the handsome young man who'd saved her. He had indeed been called a finder. Over the years, she thought perhaps she'd heard other stories, though she'd never paid much attention to them. But he was known, and he *was* royal.

Which was actually a worst-case scenario for the both of them.

"My mother was the youngest of seven princes and princesses of a very, *very* small country," he said, and she could read the reluctance in every word.

But each word was pertinent. "Regardless of her place in line, you would be an heir of something. You must have a title yourself. A *royal* title."

"I have rejected it," he returned, looking so stormy and disdainful, and yet... She knew royalty well enough, knew his story somewhat. That would have caused a ripple, and she remembered no ripples.

"Formally?" she returned. She even smiled placidly. "Or in your head when it suits you?" Because she knew plenty of lesser royals who wanted to live in both worlds. Who claimed whatever when it suited them.

She could tell by the way he crossed his arms over his chest and firmed his mouth, without saying a thing, that she'd hit the nail on the head. He didn't *wish* to be royalty, but he was, after a fashion. And hadn't cut *all* ties with that.

Which made this even more complicated than it had been. "My father will insist we marry. Perhaps I was meant for greater than minor, unknown royalty, but..." She gave her stomach a little pat. "If you take me back, this will seal both of our futures."

This did not faze Cristhian for even a moment. He lifted a large, muscled shoulder. "Perhaps *I* will insist we marry."

Her mouth dropped open at that. *"What?"*

"I haven't decided yet. This is a shock. I'll have to work through the possibilities."

He couldn't be serious. "We don't know each other. We can't…"

His gaze moved from the top of her head, all the way down to her toes and back up again. Her body throbbed with memories that had kept her warm at night for some time. She now wished she'd eradicated them rather than indulged them many a sleepless night when she'd wished to know his identity. Fantasized about a future that could include the possibility of him in it.

And now he was standing there like a jail sentence. Even if it was one that still made everything inside her buzz with a physical anticipation that did not match her internal, emotional dread.

"We know each other well enough, Princesa," he said, his voice a low scrape against the most sensitive parts of her.

But he was saying marriage was some kind of option. Returning her to her father was an option. She could only stand, mouth dropped open, air struggling to reach her lungs. Was he *insane*?

He made a shooing motion. "Go on then. Pack your things."

"I will not go back to my father," she said through gritted teeth. Her hands curled into fists. She knew she couldn't fight him. Not physically. But the desire to do so coursed through her all the same.

"Not yet. No," he agreed with annoying ease. "We have some decisions of our own to make first, but not here." He looked around her small cabin with clear distaste. "We will go to one of my estates."

"*Estates?* Tell me again you're not royalty, Cristhian."

"I am a self-made man," he returned. Then gave a grand, elegant bow, though his gaze never left hers. "I will not wait, Your Highness. We leave in thirty minutes."

CHAPTER FIVE

SHE TOOK EVERY last one of those thirty minutes, but not one second more. She did not have much, but Cristhian supposed even a runaway princess could only travel with what she could carry. He plucked the bags from her hands and marched them out to his car.

She followed him at a much slower pace. Her gait was careful, one hand placed over the rounded stomach as she stepped around icy patches in the snowy path. He had to fight the urge to cross to her and offer an arm. He prided himself on being polite in all situations, even finding missions, but it would be best for the both of them if he limited any and all physical contact that might be a dangerous reminder.

Especially since he was planning on taking her to his estate just north of Lille. Close enough to returning her, should he decide that be their fate. But also on his own turf, so *he* would be making the decisions.

It would just be the two of them and his very minimal staff. Where they could privately and safely work out some kind of…agreement. Risky, considering his body had not gotten the memo that she was his adversary now. But necessary.

Marriage? He would not be party to any more royal

tricks and maneuvers, so a union seemed like the worst-case scenario. And yet he *would* be a part of his child's life. Perhaps he'd never had any driving desire to be a father, but he knew he had wisdom to impart. He would ensure his child received that over any royal brainwashing that would no doubt come from the king.

Zia was young. Perhaps her running away meant she was not fully under her father's thumb, but Cristhian knew how this went. He had watched it play out in his mother's short life. Princesses might try to escape, but they never succeeded. They ran away instead of making a stand.

Case in point.

Moreover, Zia would not be immune from running back to Lille. She would want more for her—their—child, as his mother once had. Birthrights were dug in deep, no matter how stifling a person found the royal life.

Cristhian needed time to think. To plan. To prepare. To rearrange the world to his specifications. In a way his parents had not been able to accomplish.

Because he would not meet their fate, and he would not allow Zia to. There would be no running away, and his child would have their parents. One way or another.

He drove them to the small airport. The sky was dark, and snow had begun to fall. Takeoff would be tricky, but necessary. Once he parked, he gathered Zia's things. He could not stop himself from helping her out of the car, her slender, gloved hand sliding into his offering too many memories that threatened to distract him from his cause.

But Cristhian was stronger than that. He dropped her hand and led her into the terminal of the airport. He found his assistant.

"Is the plane ready?"

"Yes, sir. But we must take off as soon as possible. Weather is coming in. They're anticipating they'll have to lock everything down before the hour is out."

Cristhian nodded. Then followed as his assistant led them through a maze of hallways and out onto the tarmac. As they approached his plane, he handed the bags to his assistant, who would stow them away in the back of the plane.

With reluctance yet again, Cristhian offered his hand so he could help Zia up the stairs into the plane.

But she hesitated. "This plane is very small."

"An excellent quality for a plane that will land on my private airstrip."

She gave him a look, the same look she'd leveled him with inside the cabin when she'd said, "Tell me again you're not royalty, Cristhian."

But he was not. Perhaps he had an official title in Hisla, but he never used it, and the current queen—his mother's older sister—had no use for him. Nor he for her, so it worked out. Perhaps some of his estates came as an inheritance from his mother, but most of the inherited money that he'd turned into his own fortune had been from his father's movie earnings.

He thought for a moment of his grandparents in the States. His mother's family had kept them out of his childhood as best they could, but as an adult he'd forged a relationship with them. They were elderly now, his grandmother frail, his grandfather stubborn. But they would welcome news of a child.

It almost warmed him.

But there were too many complications to wade

through first. Like how he had managed to make his one and only adult mistake with a *princess*.

He helped her up the stairs and gestured her to a seat. "Take your pick and make yourself comfortable. The flight will be a few hours."

She began to follow instructions, then looked back at him as he began to duck into the cockpit.

"You're flying?" she demanded, her voice going up an octave.

He looked over his shoulder at her, eyebrow raised. "A pilot wasn't in the budget."

She scoffed. "I can only imagine what you charge for your finding services. I imagine your *budget* can include whatever you wish."

He lifted a shoulder and didn't bother to answer. "I would buckle up, Princesa. It looks like we'll be flying around some weather."

The he pushed her existence out of his mind and focused on flying.

The flight had not been smooth. Zia's nerves were shot by the time they, what felt like, skidded to a landing. She had to pry her fingers off the armrests as they were stiff from gripping so hard.

It was not Cristhian who helped her down the stairs of the plane this time, but the man he'd met at the airport. Who offered her a kind, encouraging smile, which certainly was a change of events.

She was led to another car while snow fell at heavier and heavier rates. She had no idea what country they were in, where Cristhian was taking her, and she knew she should be more concerned about that than she was, but what was there to do? He *was* the father. He had a right to some say in this.

She just had to figure out how to make sure he did not somehow have *all* the say. She had to maintain some amount of power and agency here, and she did not know how to do that just yet. She'd never had a chance to learn. Running away had always been the only answer.

She couldn't run from this, any more than she could run from the pregnancy or the fact that Cristhian was the father of her children.

Children. The most important part of all this. She would do anything for them, fight whatever powerful men she had to fight. She would have a say because she would protect them in all things. She would put their needs above all else.

The way her own mother had never stepped in and protected her or Beau. The way her father had never put anyone's needs above his country's.

She smoothed her hands over her belly, gave her children an internal promise she'd do whatever it took. To keep them safe. To keep them happy. She'd find a way.

Cristhian took the wheel of the car, his assistant not getting in with them. Zia felt a little deflated at the loss of the one person who'd offered a glimmer of kindness, but exhaustion was creeping up on her. She'd eaten on the plane, but she had not been able to sleep.

Cristhian drove them over twisting and rolling roads, the snow nearly blinding the whole way. Zia gripped the car door just as tightly as she'd held on to her seat on the airplane. Cristhian drove through it at a slow pace, and still it seemed impossible he knew where the roads were.

The snow began to ease a little. Big flakes still fell,

but not at quite the alarming rate. Cristhian slowed at a gate that after a few moments began to slowly open. He drove through it once there was enough space, then over a winding drive that led toward a…

"Cristhian."

"What?"

"This is a *castle*." Perhaps on the smaller side of many of the royal palaces she'd been to in her life, but it was still so clearly built for royalty. Stately stones, towers, intricate windows and cornices. Like a fairy tale with the snow fluttering in huge flakes all around them, and the trees and rolling ground heavy with snow.

Cristhian studied the grand building as if he'd never considered that term before. "Not a castle."

"It has *turrets*."

But he would not be deterred, because of course the man she'd been so physically attracted to she'd forgotten all sense would be the most stubborn man alive.

"Old, yes," he returned. "There's some ancient Scandinavian line to my grandmother's family. But we have never called it a castle. This is Espinas Cottage."

She snorted at the word *cottage*, but he ignored her.

"Very private. Very out of the way. We will have a few days to determine how we will move forward."

"*We* or *you*?"

He shrugged in that arrogant way of his. "Feel free to argue semantics all you like. For now, we should get in out of the cold."

Which meant he thought he was going to be making all the choices. And she was clearly stuck here—in a castle, in the middle of a blizzard, with a man who thought he ran the world.

How familiar, all in all.

And because it was familiar and frustrating, she found those old rebellions swimming around in her as he helped her walk through the snow, up grand *castle* stairs. She wanted to lash out, shock, get a leg up on all that male certainty. Just like she had as a wild, impetuous teenager who'd only ever been cowed by threats against her sister. Because her parents saw Beau's panic attacks as a weakness, a blight. Not simply a condition to be treated. For years, Zia had done whatever they wanted in the hopes they wouldn't lock Beau away.

But her sister wasn't here. The only one Zia could hurt now was herself. And *him*.

"There is something I forgot to mention," she offered as they stepped into a grand, echoing foyer.

"What's that?" he returned somewhat absently.

"I'm not having your baby, Cristhian."

He sighed heavily, disdain in every second of the sound. "Zia—"

"I am having your *babies*. Twins." And she had the great satisfaction of seeing his mouth go slack for a moment. The total and utter shock she'd put in his expression. Not put together even enough to find that blank look. Just pure, unadulterated shock.

So she smiled at him for the first time since he'd shown up in her life again, and meant that smile.

CHAPTER SIX

ZIA WAS SMUG. That self-satisfied smiled landed in his gut with a twist of fury and want, a dangerous and unfortunate combination. Because he could indulge in neither feeling that plagued him.

Twins. Two babies. It really didn't matter the number, he supposed, but it felt like a blow all the same. She *wanted* it to feel like a blow if that smile of hers was anything to go by.

So he would not react to her words. He would try not to react to her words.

"I will show you to your rooms." He sounded stiff even to his own ears, and this would not do. He could not let her know when her barbs landed. He could not show any weakness. This was too delicate. "You are no doubt exhausted. You certainly look it."

She chuckled, as if this was not an insult. "No doubt," she agreed readily. "Hungry as well."

"I will have the cook make you up a tray."

"Excellent." He led her to the stairs. Maybe the staircase was ornate. Maybe the large, uniquely shaped windows, the soaring apses, the intricate corbels and arcading gave the illusion of great elegance, but the building was a bit squat, all in all. Much of the royal accoutrements had been taken down and away before the cottage had come into his possession.

He kept it and *liked* it because it was off the beaten path. No relatives tried to "drop in" to this cottage far north of their kingdom like they did some of his other estates, usually in some effort to stir up some gossip or hard feelings. No, this was one of the few things passed down from his mother that felt like *his*.

So he would not be irritated that she insisted it had a turret, or that she wanted to keep pushing the point he was royal. It did not matter what *she* thought.

And what of King Rendall?

That was thornier, certainly, and he hadn't worked it all out yet, but he would. Once he got his more… emotional responses under control.

Twins. Not just one child, but two. It didn't really change the situation, and yet he felt changed. Like he had been able to pretend her pregnancy was simply a problem to be solved when it was just one, and now that he knew two children grew inside her they seemed more…real.

He led her up the stairs and to the first set of bedrooms he'd instructed his staff to ready. His rooms were much deeper in the castle—the *cottage*. Far, *far* away from her. He opened the door to her small guest suite.

"The rooms are readied, but my staff here is minimal, and with the snow as it is, we may be stuck that way for a time. You will have to get used to doing things on your own."

She aimed a haughty look at him. One that made him wonder how he hadn't seen *princess* written all over that elegant point of a chin. "I have been taking care of myself in a cabin on a polar island for months now, Cristhian. I am quite certain I can handle it."

"You are a princess. A few runaway attempts do not make you well-versed in roughing it, Princesa."

"I quite agree. I'm not sure spending the next few days in an understaffed castle will be the hardship you're making it out to be, but your point is taken. Though living on my own, under the detection of my father these past few months, has taught me much, I have had many cushions in this life. But with every cushion comes a condition, and sometimes those conditions are..." She trailed off, clearly struggling with a suitable word.

He could think of a few himself, but he kept his mouth resolutely closed. It would not do to relate to her. Whether it be from his own experience or his mother's.

Perhaps they would have to come to work as partners in some way to be parents to their children, but until he decided how that would work, they were adversaries. Until he set up everything exactly as he wanted it.

She never finished her sentence. He led her into the suite—a prettily appointed sitting room. The doors to the bedroom and en suite bathroom were open so she could explore. He could see her bags neatly situated along the wall.

Zia moved around the room, and he knew he should excuse himself. Inform the cook she would need some food. He should leave her, so that he could begin to enact his plans.

But the strangest thing was happening to him. No matter what forward steps he took, he couldn't decide how he wanted to proceed past tonight.

He did not know what to do.

When he was a man who always knew the next step to take. Who made quick, correct decisions in all things. He had learned it was the only way to survive with himself intact. Indecision was poison.

And currently infecting every step he took. Because he did not know what to do about *this*. About *her*.

So he hesitated, when he never hesitated. He didn't leave the room, because if he left he would have to face himself and the fact that he had no idea what his next move should be.

"What were your plans then?"

She turned to study him. "What do you mean?"

"Your plans. For you. For the babies."

Her study never stopped, but after a time she gave a little nod as if deciding to give him the truth. "In the close future, I was making the decision of where to go into labor. The island does not have the facilities for that, so you have to go to the mainland. I had some contenders. How I handled what came next would depend on how well labor went, and if I had been found out."

It was well thought out, but it was hardly the kind of thing someone could do on their own. "You must have had help."

She shrugged. And said nothing.

He had no right to be irritated by her lack of details. This was not important. What was important was what came next. "I will leave you to rest. Someone will bring some food up soon."

"And what will you be off doing?"

"Making arrangements."

"Without me?"

"It seems you have had ample time to make arrangements without *me*. Perhaps it is my turn."

She shook her head. "I am the one carrying them. I will be the one bringing them into the world. You will not shut me out of any decisions made. I will do whatever is in my power, even if it requires involving my father, to ensure that."

He was relieved that she was showing a little temper. That she was putting up a fight. He could always find his way in a fight.

"I would be careful how you threaten me with your *king*, Your Highness."

"It is not a threat," she replied, not the least bit concerned or chagrined. "It is simply explaining myself. They are my top priority. I will do whatever it takes to protect them. I am their mother."

"And I am their father."

She sighed, something in her expression softening. "I am glad you know that," she said after a moment. Then she crossed to him. Stood in front of him with wide, serious green eyes. "For all the ways we'll no doubt disagree, I *am* glad you know that."

He didn't want to believe her. He wanted to convince himself that she was simply an adept liar. He didn't know very much about her at all. She could be the most deceitful woman on the planet.

But no amount of wanting could make falsehoods a reality. Zia would no doubt lie to him at some point, but this was not a lie.

Perhaps it was a common ground to work from. Perhaps he should be glad of it, for his children's sakes. Perhaps this was some kind of hope to hold on to.

But he knew too well what hoping got a person. Where believing someone might have an interest other than their own at heart might land a person. He had learned that lesson the hard way with his mother's family. First, believing that they'd taken him from his paternal grandparents because they'd *cared*. Then, growing up knowing they didn't, being foolish enough to believe one of his cousins had befriended him out of kindness and honesty.

Instead, all Antonio had ever been doing was keeping tabs on him, all so his mother—who'd been the newly minted queen at the time—could decide how to best use him and his story for her own gain.

So Cristhian knew better than to trust. Than to believe. Than to *hope*.

Something tried to expand within him, with her standing too close. Memories knocking at the door of his mind. The way that one night had wrapped around him, held him against his will.

Even now. When he should be thinking of *anything* but the way her body might feel under his hands. The way she would taste again, here in his own world—not that fictional one they'd built that night. No, this would be real.

And unacceptable.

But she was looking up at him now as if there was something real to be salvaged, and that was her weapon. One she would no doubt wield against him if he didn't make himself clear. Right here. Right now.

"I could have you in my bed in under five minutes," he said, making certain she would feel his breath dance along her neck. "And you would do whatever I said, whatever I liked."

He saw the tremor move through her, the heat they couldn't ever share again leap into her green eyes. His own body hardened in reaction, but he would not be so easily distracted. No matter how much the potency of whatever arced between them still knocked him off his usually perfectly kept axis.

"But we are here to decide the future, Princesa. Nothing else."

And now it was *his* turn to be smug as he turned on a heel and walked out of her room.

Zia had slept well in spite of the unusual and unfortunate circumstances. She was getting more and more physically uncomfortable as the days went, but the exhaustion of lugging around two growing babies inside her always took a toll at night.

So after he'd left, no matter how frustrated and confused and worked up she'd been, hungry, too, she'd crawled into the huge, comfortable bed and fallen straight to sleep.

Unfortunately, her dreams had been…vivid. And had been less dreams and more flashes of memory. Dancing with him, the hard, hot wall he'd made. The reckless ride back to his hotel room. The sound he'd made when he'd been over her, inside her. Those dark eyes holding her gaze through it all…and how they'd been the same exact eyes to tell her he could have her in his bed in under five minutes.

So while she awoke feeling better rested, she did not

feel settled. Because even awake his words kept replaying in her head like some kind of spell.

I could have you in my bed in under five minutes. And you would do whatever I said, whatever I liked.

In spite of herself, she knew it was true, and she couldn't help but wonder just what he "liked" that might be different than that first night when they'd been strangers and under some kind of spell of their own.

But he'd only said it to put her in her place, she knew. She knew *men*, powerful men. Everything had to be their way. Everything had to be under their, what they considered, clever control. She had watched her father lash out at anyone and everyone with as many cutting remarks as he could hurl when things did not go precisely as he wanted.

So she knew Cristhian's parting shot had been launched because he did not feel in control. And *that* at least gave her some satisfaction.

He didn't know what to do with her, with this, and it was gratifying because she hadn't known what to do at first, either.

But right now she was too hungry to consider her next steps beyond food. She changed her clothes quickly and then stopped short in the sitting room. A platter with an array of baked goods sat on one of the little tables.

She settled herself in the chair and polished off two before she'd taken more than a breath or two. Immediately, she felt better. She considered a third, and then thought better of it. She drank a glass of water—it was cold as though it had been ice water a time ago, but the ice had melted.

She had no idea what time it was. She couldn't find a

clock in these rooms, and her phone had died sometime in the night. She plugged it in, waited for it to boot up, then sent Beau a little text message that she had left the island, that she was fine, and more information would be forthcoming.

Beau wouldn't love that, but it was the best Zia could offer until she knew what the next steps were going to be. Certainly not be carted back to Lille by Cristhian, but if Cristhian's alternatives involved something she didn't think was best for the children, she might be forced to go back to her father and ask for his help.

Her stomach sank, hard and painful at the thought. That eventuality would not be protecting her children, because whatever her father could do for her, for them, it would only be in service to Lille.

Which meant, likely, a marriage to Cristhian either way. Some kind of insulting agreement with his mother's family. No choice. Her children treated like little dolls or robots, unable to have their own feelings or flaws.

Just the thought filled her with the kind of anxiety that could not be good for her children. These were all ifs and worst-case scenarios. She shouldn't get too far ahead of herself. She had to deal with this step by practical step. Just like she had been since she'd finally made that choice to disappear.

She wished she could talk to Beau, but they had deemed phone conversations too dangerous. Too easily tracked and found. She would have to work this out on her own, with just the occasional text message from an unmarked number.

She blew out a breath. She could do it. She'd been doing it all these months. But first she needed something more than a pastry. She left her room, followed the hall-way to the grand staircase Cristhian had led her up last night. Downstairs, she poked around in empty rooms until she found what appeared to be a dining room. Nar-row, but long, a table mimicking the room in the center…

With Cristhian sitting at the head of it. A plate of food in front of him at one side, a laptop at the other. His dark hair was a little damp, like he'd just emerged from a shower not that long ago, and he was dressed casually in a sweater and soft-looking pants.

Her heart felt as though it tripped over itself in her chest. She did not know how one man could be so hand-some. She might keep pointing out that he was royalty no matter how little he liked it, but he didn't look it. He was so tall and broad, muscular as though he did a lot of labor. He must have taken after his American father.

No doubt another sore subject. Because she'd remem-bered belatedly that his parents had died in a very famous car accident. She had been too young to remember the actual event, but it had still been discussed as she'd been growing up. One of those tragedies people whispered about, hoping if they expressed enough dismay at lives cut too short, it wouldn't happen to them.

It was so strange how all the facets of him were un-furling in the here and now after she'd convinced herself he was just a phantom in her life, never to return. But she hadn't let herself think much about the reality of the babies she would one day hold. She was struck with the thought now. Who would they look like? Would they have his dark eyes, or some mix of her green?

She had wanted to be surprised about the sex, because

the truth was it was too much to think about the babies as *people* when he hadn't been in her life.

And now he was…sort of. She had no idea how it would play out, but it made everything feel all the more real.

"Good morning," he said, somewhat absently, without lifting his gaze. As if he'd known she was standing there taking stock all along. "We are well and truly snowed in. We do not anticipate being able to dig out for at least forty-eight hours. I suggest you make yourself comfortable in whatever ways you can, and certainly let the staff know if you require anything." He made a broad gesture. "Sit. Ramon will bring you out a plate."

She wanted to eat, but the need to be contrary was too deep-seated to ignore. "I ate some of the food left for me upstairs."

He nodded. "And now you will sit and eat some protein."

A man with a plate appeared as if on cue. He placed it at the seat next to Cristhian, who gave the man a sharp look that the man ignored.

Zia raised an eyebrow, surprised to read how little Cristhian wanted her to sit next to him written all over his face.

Well, that was enough to get her feet moving and to settle herself into the seat next to him. She flashed a smile at the retreating man, and then her breakfast companion.

He did not react in any way, except to look at his laptop.

Her plate was full of a large omelet, which looked delicious. She'd cut out coffee for the duration of her pregnancy, so she was grateful for the large glasses of juice and water at her plate. Though she wouldn't mind a warm beverage later. The room was warm, but she could practically feel the cold from outside pressing against the walls of the *castle*.

She took a few bites of her breakfast, then studied the man seated next to her. "Have you informed my father you've found me?" She genuinely didn't know what he would have done last night. On the one hand, he seemed fully…himself. The kind of man who would take orders from no one and would do exactly as he pleased.

On the other hand, he took these jobs of finding people, so he must have *some* deference to the people paying him.

There was a slight hesitation from Cristhian. Nothing in his expression changed. He didn't move. But she sensed just the hint of…something. Not discomfort, because the man seemed endlessly comfortable in every situation. But something akin to it.

"I will make my decisions about how to proceed before I report to your father," he said at length. His posture and his delivery stiff.

Interesting. She took another bite of the delicious omelet and watched Cristhian. "And you have yet to make those decisions?"

His expression changed. Hardened ever so slightly.

It was no mystery why she'd allowed herself a nameless night with this man. He was too handsome for anyone's own good. It didn't matter if it was that sly smile and easy flirtations of their first meeting, or that hard, angry demeanor. It *all* did something to her.

Something she was going to have to learn how to control. She had always been a bit…spiteful. Not her best quality, but she didn't like to be told what to do—a problem as a princess who was constantly being told what to do. She hid her contradictory nature better than Beau, but it was still a struggle. When someone told her something she *should*, it automatically made her want to not.

She supposed that was why her father had learned the only way to get through to her was to threaten Beau's future. Spite never held up in the face of protecting her sister from the possibilities her father used like a bludgeon. Private asylums. Medical interventions she certainly didn't need. Anything that made it seem like Beau's hardships were something she should be ashamed of.

Zia wouldn't allow it. Beau claimed she had everything under control at the moment, and Zia had to believe her, but there was still the possibility that how Cristhian handled this with the king would reflect back on what Father did to Beau.

So Zia *should not* want to sleep with Cristhian ever again. She shouldn't be the least bit interested in his bed or what he would want to do in it. His arrogant little quip last night should have cured her of all her lust.

But it decidedly had not.

Until he spoke his next words. "Once my doctor is able to make the trip, we will do a paternity test."

CHAPTER SEVEN

CRISTHIAN HAD BEEN careful not to look too much in Zia's direction since she'd appeared. There was a danger in her beauty, in the way those fluffy sweaters hugged the fascinating bump she'd grown since he'd last seen her.

So he didn't look at her for more than the briefest of seconds, until he'd delivered his current challenge. Her eyes went wide, her mouth a little slack. He'd certainly shocked her. She blinked once, and when she spoke it wasn't with that haughtiness she'd come into the dining room with this morning.

"You brought me here and you don't believe me?" she asked, sounding…younger and more hurt than she had any right to.

He could let her think that he didn't believe her. He *wanted* to let her think that. But every time his mercenary instincts wanted to take over, he was reminded of his parents. Of the way they had worked together—no matter all their outside problems—to ensure he was safe and well.

His parents *had* loved each other, so it was different, but everything he had been able to rise above had been because they had started his life out in a safe, loving place.

He wanted the same for his children, and that meant he could not be cruel to their mother, even when it would be a solid weapon to use to save himself.

But that made every step he took more complicated than he was used to. There was no clear enemy here. For all Zia represented a complicated issue, she was not like his mother's family trying to use him. The paths ahead were all thorny. And he did not doubt his ability to maneuver through them and come out on top. He was just uncomfortable with the time and care it would take to accomplish the perfect, controlled outcome. One that did not leave him open to being used. One that did not result in rash decisions to run away, and the punishments that came from that.

So sometimes he would have to give her the truth. Even when he didn't want to.

"It is not about belief. It is about everything legal that will plague us. Inheritances, trusts, titles." He wanted to blame her for bringing those things to the table, but she was a little too on the nose about all the royal things he disdained…but hadn't formally denounced. That had been the deal he'd struck with his aunt. That had been the condition in getting his freedom, his own life.

Most days, he considered that a great win. Standing up, not running away. It grated that in the face of Zia it felt less a win and more a concession.

His feelings, however, did not matter. Only settling this did. "We will need to have incontrovertible proof that our children are biologically ours in order to move forward."

She swallowed at that, and he had to look away from the way her emotions chased across her face. They had to work together in order to make the world a safe place for their children, but that did not mean he needed to concern himself with her *feelings*.

"I suppose that makes sense. But you said we'd be stuck here for at least forty-eight hours."

"Yes."

"What shall we do in the meantime?"

It wasn't meant to be flirtatious. He could tell by the way her gaze was on her food, the way she didn't offer him any sultry looks. But when he didn't respond right away, when he let the silence settle after her question, she must have realized what it sounded like. Because her cheeks turned a faint shade of pink.

She cleared her throat. "What I mean is, how do you entertain yourself in this large castle? *Alone*." She tacked on the last word forcefully enough he could not quite resist the slight curve of his mouth.

"Did I say I spend a lot of time here *alone*?" he returned, when that's exactly what he did. Of all his estates, this was the one he considered his personal, private sanctuary, when he wanted nothing to do with the world around him.

It was happenstance it was his closest holding to her home country, which was why he'd brought her here. Geography.

She sighed. "I suppose you have a parade of women littered at every spot. Women do love a prince."

He knew she was poking at him, and yet he couldn't stop himself from scowling.

Her smile went sharp, delight in a barb landed. That look shouldn't hit him like a blow, knocking enough sense out of him he remembered all too clearly what she tasted like.

"However," she continued, "unless you have someone locked away in an attic, I believe we—and your minimal staff—are all that are here in the moment. So what do you suggest we do for the next forty-eight hours? Get to know one another?"

"I thought we were *well* acquainted, Zia."

She rolled her eyes. "Perhaps it is worth mentioning that there are many things I shouldn't do in my condition."

He could ignore her meaning. He probably *should* ignore her. But he couldn't help himself. "Is that pointed, Zia?"

Her gaze didn't flutter. She didn't look away from him. She lifted her chin, all royal and dignified. But he had seen her *very* undignified, and that memory served neither of them.

He indulged it all the same.

"Does it need to be pointed, Cristhian?"

He lifted a shoulder. Did his best to embody a casual carelessness he didn't exactly feel at the moment. "What is it you want to know then?"

She rested her chin on her fist as if she took that question very seriously. "Who were you raised by after your parents died?"

He wasn't sure what he expected, but not that, and he did not care for the way it made him feel like he was backed into a corner, in a defensive position. Particularly when it was clear she was curious, not starting some kind of war.

Pretending the answer meant more than it did would

no doubt give her ammunition for whatever battles lay ahead, so he spelled it out as nonchalantly as he could manage.

"I bounced around family. They had a lot of it."

"They? Not you?"

"My father's family was interested, but American and less powerful when it came to things like citizenships and titles. My mother's family was not the biggest proponent of her marriage. I was…a problem to be solved more than anything, but an heir of sorts, whether they liked it or not. And a convenient story to trot out when they wanted attention."

"I have found that you do not have to be the result of a disdained marriage to be considered a problem to be solved."

Cristhian studied her as she finished the last bite of her breakfast. "You are a princess. An heir. What's the problem?"

"I had more interest in playing football than learning protocol. I was much better at sneaking around the rules than following them. I need…ed freedom and fresh air, and there is little of that to be had while growing up a princess. My sister would have been better suited, I think, to some of it, but…" She shrugged her shoulders.

"You are older?" he prompted when she said nothing more. He could have found this information out himself, but in his work he found the stories people told themselves, and then shared, offered more information than facts did.

"No. Beau is actually three minutes older. But since there were two of us, my parents got to choose who would be considered the heir. They held it over our heads like a prize, but neither of us were too eager to win it."

"Then how did you get chosen?"

"I was deemed prettier. Easier to mold. My sister… She has a head for details. She could recite protocol back to you better than even my father. But…" She shook her head, and the smile on her face was found even though she was explaining her own demise. "You cannot threaten or manipulate Beaugonia. She will do as she will. I…did not like the consequences my parents threatened me with, so I learned to pretend better than she did. And so I was chosen."

She leaned forward then, a serious, intent look on her face. When she spoke, it was with a quiet, careful fervor. "If I am returned to my father, he will insist we marry. Since you are royal, we will be named heirs to his throne. Me as queen, you as something. And we will be told to make the same choices with our children. Well, unless one is a boy and one is a girl. Guess who gets chosen then."

He did not like the picture she painted at all, but he also had infinite confidence that if he did return her to King Rendall, Cristhian would find a way to get what *he* wanted out of the arrangement. She wouldn't sway his opinion of what must be done, of what would be best. So what struck him in the moment was her *unless one is a boy*.

"You do not know the sex of the babies?"

She sat back in her chair, rested her hands over that swell of her stomach. "I wanted to be surprised," she returned, so primly and without meeting his gaze that he knew there was more to that story than she was giving him at the moment.

But he would know it eventually.

"The doctor will tell us. So that we can make the appropriate plans."

She eyed him then, with a disdain he didn't care to admit made him want to fidget.

Unheard of.

"It does not matter their sex. They will not be heirs to anything. I will not imprison my children."

"Come, Princesa, surely you're not so dramatic as to liken *prison* to the privilege and opportunity you were raised with."

"I try to tell myself that. I try to be grateful for all that I have, but, Cristhian, do you have any idea what it's like to know everything you are is a mismatch for the life you are expected to lead? And so the entirety of that life stretching out before you will be nothing but a farce. For someone else. Never yourself."

He didn't scowl at her, though he wanted to. "So many people concerned with themselves, and so little concern for the people who must deal with the fallout of their actions."

The rejoinder didn't seem to land as he'd hope it might. She tilted her head and studied him, as though she could see straight through. When no one saw straight through.

Not even yourself.

He pushed that thought away as she spoke.

"You see, the difference here is, I can acknowledge the great privilege you were brought up with, and still imagine that losing your parents, being bounced around without love, was difficult for you." She stood then, and he couldn't quite take his gaze from the pregnant belly. Where his children grew inside her. *His*.

Children who would not be bounced around. Who would feel love, and not have it ripped away from them by fate.

"I can have empathy for you, no matter the circumstance, Cristhian. I consider that a gift."

He looked up at her then, at those green eyes. And he knew what he must do. "I must thank you for this little speech. It has given me clarity on how we will move forward."

She raised an eyebrow. "Oh?"

"The moment we can get a minister here, we will be married."

Zia wondered if she'd had some kind of cardiac event. She was standing, but she couldn't feel her legs. Her breath didn't come in and out as it should.

"I beg your pardon?" she managed.

"We will marry," he repeated, pushing out of the chair himself. "There is no other way that truly gives our children the childhood I want them to have. Bouncing around is a no go for me, and a life without their mother would also not do."

"What about a life without their father?"

"You should have hidden better if you wished for that."

"Better than an isolated arctic island shrouded by polar night?" she demanded, facing off with him as if they were in a boxing ring rather than a posh dining room.

He smiled at her then, and she had to wonder what was wrong with her that his smile could still send a shimmer of sparks through her when he was being the most ridiculous man alive.

"Unfortunately for you, Zia, I would have found you anywhere."

Which might have been romantic if he'd been the one looking for her. But no, it had been her father. Cristhian had no doubt forgotten about her the morning she'd disappeared. Hopped in the next bed and so on and so forth for the past seven months.

Which was reason enough to stop this right here, right now. "I will not marry you."

"I did not ask. You said it yourself. Your father will insist we marry should I return you to him. I cannot really be insisted upon, if I do not agree, but in this case, it is the best-case scenario."

"To marry a veritable stranger so we don't have to work out a custody agreement?"

He considered this, or more likely pretended to. Then he shrugged. "Yes."

She shook her head. She had known he wouldn't be reasonable, but she didn't think he'd be this. "This is ridiculous. You clearly haven't thought this through at all."

"On the contrary, I've done nothing but think since I was met with this." He gestured at her stomach. "The options are limited with our complicated backgrounds. We must marry and prepare a united front against all that will come. We are not enemies, Zia. We will work out what is best for the children. Together."

But he didn't say that like some kind of promise of compromise and reason. He said it like *together* meant her trotting along after him, doing whatever he wished. And that was exactly what she'd escaped.

She wouldn't go back. Her children would be raised to be strong and independent and not victims to other people's whims or power. She knew what it was like. To endure it. To watch other people endure it. She wanted more for them. So much more.

"Perhaps I am not your enemy, Cristhian, but you are turning into mine."

He chuckled at that. *Chuckled.* She wanted to slap him.

"What is it you think a marriage should be that we could not accomplish? If we are both reasonable, we can make all important decisions as a team. We have many estates to choose from. We can be as involved or as not involved in Lille as you wish. It's actually the perfect answer to all your problems."

"Is it?"

"You were all set to marry that duke or what have you?"

She didn't believe for a second he didn't know exactly who she'd been set to marry. "A crown prince," she bit out.

"Ah, of course. Were you desperately in love with him? Did you know each other well? My guess is no if you so willingly went to my bed all those months ago."

She had no argument for that. She had met Lyon Traverso all of twice. And they'd never been alone together. He'd shown about as much interest in her as he'd shown in the salmon that had been served at dinner.

"So, what is the difference?" Cristhian asked, with a kind of patience she didn't trust at all. "Rank?" he asked silkily.

"It has nothing to do with rank." He wanted to paint

her some spoiled, ignorant, materialistic princess, and maybe she should let him. Maybe it would take this ridiculous idea of marriage off the table.

"Then what does it have to do with?" he asked, with an innocence so ludicrous she was tempted to chuckle herself.

"It has to do with the fact I have a right to…make my own decisions. To be free of yet another man who wants me to follow along, regardless of my own thoughts or opinions or fears. I knew what I was getting into with the arranged marriage." Protecting her sister if nothing else, but now she had children to protect. "I don't know what I'm getting into with you, Cristhian, and I will not put myself through that simply because *you* think it's the best course of action, when *I* know it's not."

All his casual masks melted off his face in that moment. His mouth got very hard, very serious. His eyes all dark flame and intensity, which reminded her of things it shouldn't when he looked as angry as he had when his gaze had met hers through the window back in her cabin.

But her body couldn't seem to tell the difference between anger and heat. Fury and lust. They seemed all tangled up together low in her belly, in the heaviness of her breasts.

When he stepped closer, she had to internally remind herself to breathe. Not lean in.

"One thing I will make sure of, Zia, regardless of you, is that these children will come first. Your whims are immaterial."

Whims. He really was the most frustrating and infuriating man she could have made this mistake with. "My whims?" She gestured at the castle around them. "What about yours? They seem to be winning."

"*I* am thinking about what's best for the children. *You* keep talking about yourself."

Perhaps that's what it sounded like to him. She couldn't even quite blame him for thinking that was what she meant. Even if it poked at her so that everything seemed to deflate. Exhaustion crept in, tears trying to find purchase in her eyes, though she fought them.

She could explain it to him. What it was like to watch a mother bow and scrape to a father who had all the control. She could tell him what it felt like as a young girl to watch her mother whisper truths, but always, *always* capitulate to her father's orders and mandates. No matter what she told her daughters. She could tell him in no uncertain terms she wanted more for her children. A mother who they could be proud of, who they could trust.

That all the things she desired for herself were really for them. And so much she'd done before this pregnancy had been for Beau, not herself. Because for all Beau's strong personality, her panic attacks left her vulnerable. She'd needed a protector. Zia had the ability to be that. Just like she had the ability, the *requirement* to be her children's staunchest supporter. This was love, above all else, she believed. Sacrificing everything to protect those who needed it.

But he couldn't possibly understand. He wanted her to be the selfish, pampered princess. And so, in his mind, she always would be. So it was with her father, so it was with no doubt every man.

"Well, Cristhian, this *self* you're so disdainful of will have to say *I do* for you to force me into marriage. So unless you have mastered brainwashing or ventriloquism, I think we are at an impasse." And with that, she turned on a heel and left his grand dining room and his fuming expression.

CHAPTER EIGHT

CRISTHIAN DIDN'T FUME for long. He knew how to deal with selfish, childish royalty. Let her throw her tantrums. Let her storm out of every room in this place.

He would come out on top. He'd spent his morning after breakfast lining up a minister to arrive once the roads were passable. He'd had a long call with his lawyer about all the necessary legalities of naming heirs of his own fortune.

They would deal with her family…after a time. Because he still had not determined the right approach to King Rendall. According to Zia, he would want the same thing Cristhian wanted: a marriage. Admittedly, in the privacy of his own head, Cristhian didn't love the idea of wanting the same thing as a king, but it was the only plausible option to give his children the family they deserved.

Zia could worry about *her* freedom, *her* whims, *her* selfish desires all she wanted. *He* would not be swayed. Their children would have the support of two parents, no matter what Cristhian had to threaten to accomplish it. They would have the options of the best of everything. But most of all, they would receive the same foundation Cristhian had received.

Which meant he was in charge. He did not have to convince Zia to follow his way. She would simply follow it or…lose.

What, he did not know yet, but he would use whatever means he wished to protect his children, and their mother, no matter how selfish she might be. And now that he had the practicalities out of the way, and nothing to do but wait for the snow to stop, he called his grandparents.

He decided on a video call, as he wanted to see their faces when they reacted to the news. He'd taught them how to answer one on their phones, but that didn't necessarily mean they would manage. Still, after a few rings, his grandmother's face appeared on his screen.

"Did we do it right?" his grandmother asked, squinting at him.

"If you can hear me."

"Yes, we've got it. Well, now. To what do we owe this out-of-the-blue call?" His grandfather looked older every time Cristhian got on a video call with them. It was a sad mark of time, and yet one his parents had never gotten to enjoy. So Cristhian tried to be grateful for what he had in them.

"I have a bit of announcement. I am to be married."

"Cristhian!" His grandmother clapped her hands together in delight. "We didn't know you were seeing anyone. You haven't even brought her to visit." It was a scolding, but it was wrapped up in love and joy for what his grandmother no doubt thought a happy occasion.

He wouldn't take that idea from them, but he couldn't outright lie about it either. "It is…complicated."

"Ah," his grandfather said in that world wise way of

his. "The kind of complicated that will make us great-grandparents?"

His grandfather had always known how to get right to the point, and even though it twisted something tangled inside him, he smiled. "Yes."

"Oh," his grandmother said, so desperately trying to hide her disappointment with enthusiasm. "Well, aren't we lucky? To have lived this long. You'll bring everyone to meet us, won't you?"

"Of course. Once we are able." His grandparents nodded along, not letting any disdain show through. They never had, no matter what he'd done. "Zia is having twins."

"Twins? Twins! Robert, do we have any twins in the family?"

"My grandmother was a twin!" his grandfather all but shouted, pride in every word.

Cristhian smiled in spite of himself. "Zia is a twin herself."

"That's excellent. She'll know just how to raise them then. Oh, two great-grandbabies. Aren't we lucky?" His grandmother beamed over at Grandfather. Disappointment over the nontraditional circumstances quickly and easily left behind.

Cristhian should feel relieved or warmed by their excitement, but there was a strange kind of discomfort twirling around inside him. He couldn't put his finger on what was causing it, so he just pushed the conversation forward.

"I wanted you to know as it is likely to move forward… quickly. I will keep you updated, of course."

His grandparents nodded, then looked at each other

in that way they had that spoke of some internal communication no one else was privy to.

"May we offer some advice?" his grandmother asked gently. Because she was a gentle woman. Too gentle, perhaps, for the world she'd been thrust into. A famous son. The slings and arrows of their daughter-in-law's family in the aftermath of such loss.

And yet she had never taken any of that out on Cristhian himself. He held this as a personal guidepost. These people on the screen in front of him, so unlike the world he lived in, and yet, the exact guide he wanted.

"Of course."

"Your parents loved each other very much," Grandmother said with a heavy wistfulness and a look away from the screen, no doubt at one of the many pictures she kept of his father.

"Yes, I know."

She turned back to the screen. "It was the foundation, and why you're such a good man, despite such…trials."

He could not quite manage the smile he knew his grandmother wanted. He had not set out to be *good*, per se, and the thought she might think it settled in a bit like guilt.

"And your father was a good man for the same reason," Grandfather said firmly. "Love is always the foundation. If you'd take any advice from us, we hope it's that. With love as a foundation, no matter the tragedies life throws at you, you'll find a way to endure."

Cristhian did not want any more tragedies, but he knew his grandparents spoke of their own. One they had weathered, with love.

No, Cristhian didn't care for that advice, but it was…

interesting. So he smiled. Chatted some more about people his grandparents knew. He let them tell all their stories from church, the beauty parlor, the grain elevator coffee shop. These things were foreign in Cristhian's life, but his grandparents always made it sound like a world he could step into if he ever needed.

Like the foundation his parents had built him, his grandparents had offered an escape hatch—once he'd been old enough to rid himself of his mother's family's royal shenanigans. He'd never taken it, still didn't want to, but something about it being there…meant something.

He tried not to think about Zia, talking about her royal prison. Perhaps she had not been afforded an escape hatch, but she'd found one, hadn't she? And still, the way he saw it, she cared for her own wants more than their children's needs.

But his grandparents had raised a good man by loving each other. His parents, the same, if he was to be counted a good man. So, Cristhian supposed, that was the answer to his trouble.

Love.

He would simply make Zia fall in love with him. Then all would fall into place. And be well.

After a post-breakfast nap, Zia felt slightly more herself. She still thought Cristhian was a ridiculous ogre, but she was reminded she had the strength and cleverness to outmaneuver her father. What was Cristhian but a slightly different version of that?

She just needed to pace herself. To think. And didn't this blizzard that had them stuck here without doctors or ministers give her just that kind of time?

She considered her phone. A missive to Beau would help her think through her options, but it was still risky. Beau was clever enough to outmaneuver their father and his men, but Cristhian complicated things. He was certainly smarter than Father's men, considering he'd been the only one capable of finding Zia, which meant he might be Beau's match in terms of sneakiness.

If she needed to escape him, too, she would need to do it without putting Beau in the crosshairs of it all. She would need to do it without anyone. She would have to rely on herself.

So, she decided the first step was to explore the castle. Get to know it. She knew better than most that a good escape required an excellent understanding of the landscape you were living in. She did not have the benefit of growing up here to know the nooks and crannies of where to hide and where to bolt.

So that was her first mission.

She left her room, but instead of taking the usual stairs down, she walked deeper into the hallway upstairs.

It wasn't quite like the castle she'd grown up in. The architecture was rather similar, but there were no royal portraits. No cases or walls of heirlooms. Everything was rather bare. But there were grand windows—some with beautiful stained-glass scenes, some floor-to-ceiling looking out over the estate around the castle.

Outside the world was nothing but bright, expansive white. She could almost believe they'd been snowed in here forever. It looked and felt like some kind of fairy tale out there.

Except here she was, trapped with the villain rather than the hero.

She sighed. She shouldn't think of him as either. The truth was, no matter what happened, Cristhian *was* her children's father. And she didn't know enough about him as a person to determine him a villain in that respect.

She didn't consider her own father a villain, either. The idea of him being her adversary really gave him too much credit. He was simply…self-absorbed. He could be cruel, but only when it suited his purposes—his purpose was running a kingdom. She figured all men probably fit that mold, but she wasn't yet sure what purpose Cristhian was acting under.

Since he did not have a kingdom to run, maybe she could find some inner core of reason inside him. Maybe if she got a better sense of *him*, she would know how to handle all this. How to maneuver.

Or how to escape.

She did not know if this castle meant anything to Cristhian when he was a man with *estates*. If it did, perhaps it would give some insight into his character, so she continued her exploration. Poking her head into any and every room. A library, an office that looked unused, a few generic bedrooms that had most of the furniture under coverings.

About halfway down the hall, she found a gorgeous conservatory. She spent the better part of thirty minutes there, enjoying the sunlight and beautiful green in contrast to all the white outside. So far, it was her favorite room.

Of course *her* favorite didn't matter, she reminded herself when she was tempted to curl up in the chair and doze. She was on a mission. So, with reluctance, she left the sunny room and went back into the hallway that now felt chilly in comparison. More covered up, unused rooms greeted her as she made her way around the curve of the hallway.

Once she made it to the almost complete other side of the castle, she found a suite of rooms that she had the sneaking suspicion were Cristhian's. She almost didn't notice it at first, because the decor in the room was as bare as the halls. It could be any guest room, anywhere, but none of the furniture was covered up, and there were little signs of life in the sitting room.

A folded-up newspaper on an end table, a jacket hung on the back of a chair. There was a computer cord coiled on a desk in the corner, missing its laptop.

Perhaps that should have been a sign to stop her perusal—no doubt Cristhian was a private man—but instead she pushed forward. Into a sprawling bedroom. The bed was huge; the windows that looked over yet more snow dominated one wall. There was no art on the walls, just a beautiful wallpaper that reminded Zia of the blue back on the island when polar night had just begun to lift.

She saw nothing personal in the whole expanse of a sleeping area, until her gaze landed on a large dresser. On top, a framed picture. Zia moved closer.

It was a wedding portrait of two outrageously gorgeous people. Then it dawned on her.

His late parents.

Cristhian looked almost exactly like the man she believed to be his father. A movie star, if she recalled correctly. The only real difference she could note from the picture was Cristhian had more of his mother's darker coloring than the blond and blue-eyed star.

Zia still couldn't remember what country his mother

was from, but she'd look it up once she was back in her room. Maybe that would be a clue in to him as well. Maybe if she got a better handle on the people who'd made him, she'd have a better handle on *him*.

She snorted, alone in his bedroom, because the idea of handling him was so ridiculous. From that very first moment in the bar, her gaze meeting his, she hadn't been able to handle him or what he brought out in her.

But things were different now. They had to be. She smoothed a hand over her stomach, her babies, dancing around in there as if already jostling for space in whatever rooms they entered. She wanted to give them all the space they deserved. She wanted to give them *everything*.

Which wasn't all that different than what Cristhian had said this morning. Maybe there was some common ground to be found. If they both wanted what was best for their children, there was room for a lot of common ground.

But it wouldn't be in marriage. It couldn't be.

Zia looked at the two happy people in the wedding portrait and wondered if that happiness was real or the illusion of a picture. Did happiness with another person exist? Or did it always sour into what her parents shared?

One person wielding all their power over the other. Then either fighting, or her mother's head bowed acquiescence.

Zia wanted neither for her babies.

On a sigh, she turned and left the room. The only real insight gained from the upstairs was that Cristhian either didn't care about decor, or he didn't care much about or spend much time at this castle, and that he had truly loved his parents.

Zia wondered, perhaps unfairly, if it was easy to love parents who had died before you were even a teenager.

She lumbered downstairs, pressing a hand to her stomach. The more she was on her feet, the heavier she felt most days. When she'd been back at the cabin, she had always had ample sitting time. She should likely take a break from her exploring, but she didn't want to sit with inaction and her thoughts right now. So she pressed on.

But she didn't get far. After skipping the dining room since she'd already been familiarized with that, and then poking her head into what had turned out to be some linen closet of some kind, she came to a room with two grand doors open. It was some kind of sitting room, all dark woods and warm colors, with sunlight dappling the plush carpet. It was the kind of room meant for cozy nights and long, meaningful conversations.

A fire crackled in the hearth, and Cristhian sat in an oversize chair, a newspaper spread out in front of him.

She wanted to step back, not let him see her, but he looked up, those dark eyes meeting hers. She still could not quite prepare herself for the way her body reacted to his gaze taking her in. She wanted to be immune, but it always felt like his hands on her again, and no matter how she felt about him rationally, her body was apparently the least rational part of this whole package.

It would revel in his hands on her again, even in this state. Even with her brain telling her to get it together. And she didn't back away or excuse herself. She stepped deeper into the warm, cozy room.

But then his mouth curved into a welcoming smile,

not sharp or flirtatious at all. Just kind. *This* she did not trust at all.

"Come. Sit." He gestured at a table full of food. "Are you hungry?"

She shouldn't join him, she knew, but the room smelled like heaven, and she *was* hungry again. Walking around had worked up an appetite.

There was a large chair that matched his on the other side of the table, so she walked over without saying a word and settled herself in it. There were trays of fruit, cheeses, little pastries, all arranged artfully. There were three pitchers, one filled with water, the other two filled with juices. She shouldn't let herself get used to this kind of luxury. If she was going to find her way in this, she was no doubt going to be back to square one at some point. A small cabin, an isolated island. Just her.

And your babies.

She glanced at Cristhian, who was watching her fill her plate. Was there anywhere she could run away to that he would not find? She had the sinking suspicion the answer was no.

So you will just have to figure out a way to get through to him, Zia.

It felt like an impossible task, but she couldn't believe in impossible. Not when it came to her children. Everything had to be possible, if she just worked hard enough.

But first, she was going to eat her fill. She curled up in the big chair and took bites of everything. "Your cook is exceptional," she said in between pastries.

"Yes, I make a habit of exceptional."

She shouldn't find that charming. It shouldn't make

her smile. He was arrogant and ridiculous and that was never a good combination.

"Did you enjoy your tour of the castle?" he asked. Blandly.

But she stopped midchew, because she had not been aware of anyone who might have seen her snooping about. And still he knew. Or was pretending to.

So she pretended she didn't care what he knew. "It was very informative. I cannot decide if you have an aversion to art and any of the touches that might make a *castle* a home, or if this simply isn't a space you spend much time in."

He seemed to consider this by looking around the room they were in. Which, in fairness, had art. Books. Nothing *too* personal, though.

"The cottage was stripped before it came into my possession," he said after a moment. His gaze returned to his newspaper.

"Stripped?" Zia echoed, not quite understanding his meaning.

"I may have royal blood, as you like to point out, but no one in my mother's family is too keen on that truth. They prefer to use me or manipulate me, whatever makes them feel powerful. So while my aunt insisted I keep my title and take on Espinas Cottage, she made sure anything not bolted down was taken back to their royal seats that surely deserved such heirlooms."

He said this without any bitterness. Like it was just a fact and it mattered not at all to him. But it had to matter, didn't it? Not the things themselves, but the fact his own family would treat him as an outsider.

She did not care for being one of her family, of having

her whole life defined by how well she upheld the Rendall legacy, but she could not imagine being young and orphaned and then feeling as though she did not belong.

Did he have no emotion about that? Or had the years allowed him to heal from it?

These were things that were dangerous for her to wonder, even more dangerous for her to know. She had to keep her wits about her if she was to ensure her freedom.

Something she struggled to remember when he lowered his paper and met her gaze with his dark one. His mouth subtly curved, the firelight giving his skin a burnished gold look about it. Like he'd be warm and safe to the touch.

Be stronger, Zia.

"Your cabin on that island wasn't exactly full of knick-knacks."

"I ran away in the dead of night. To a polar island with limited resources. If I had access to home decor, I would have certainly bought some. But my focus was on not being detected and keeping these two healthy." She rested her hands on her belly.

His gaze followed them. "What made you choose that island for your escape?" he asked, his gaze remaining on her stomach.

She studied him with suspicion. Why did he care? What was he trying to get out of her? Would he use her answer against her in some way? File away everything she said so he could follow her inevitable escape?

But he was looking at their children, essentially. Even if he couldn't see them, that was why he was studying her stomach. He was thinking about *children*. And maybe if they could both realize that these two were the most important thing, and the adults in the situation weren't sworn enemies, they could come to some reasonable conclusions and agreements.

She had to believe that. "I saw a video. I liked the idea of polar night. Of being able to hide away in months of darkness while I figured out what to do."

"You did not find this polar night...depressing?"

She smiled a little, even though she shouldn't let her guard down like this. "No. It was...cozy. I like being on my own. Deciding each day what I want to do. It was especially important to be alone to make the decisions I needed to make."

Something in his expression darkened, but he made no scathing remark. His attention went back to his newspaper. But she began to wonder if he was even reading it, or if it was just a prop. If this was all just an act.

"I do not know what you think you're doing, but you're hardly going to butter me up with sweets and change my mind about everything."

His eyebrow rose as he slowly set the newspaper aside and then turned to her. "I do not wish to change your mind. The marriage will go through regardless of how you feel about it."

She could have groaned, but she needed to resist those urges. Take a page out of his book and offer nothing but a calm, impenetrable sense of right.

She leaned forward, as comfortably as she could with her belly right there. She tried to sound calm and rational instead of accusatory. "Let me ask you something, then. Why do you think marriage is the right choice? You clearly have not watched two people make each other miserable at the cost of their children."

"No, I have not. Nor will we."

She wished she could believe it would be that easy. But she had seen too much. "Just because we don't love each other doesn't mean there won't be hard feelings. It certainly doesn't mean there won't be battles of our wills. I would like to avoid such things. Perhaps you don't understand. Perhaps I haven't been clear. I truly did not tell you because I was so focused on…making certain my family did not know that I did not think of how to track you down. It was not my intention to cut you out. If we can find a way to keep my identity unknown, I am happy to share custody in a careful, fair way."

"Perhaps *you* don't understand. We might not love each other now, but this does not mean we can't."

Zia laughed. The sound bubbled up and right out of her.

But Cristhian did not laugh at what had to be a joke as well. He did not smile. He did not wink.

He just sat there, looking at her placidly, as if he was serious.

Clearly he'd lost his mind.

Or she had lost hers.

CHAPTER NINE

THE SHOCK ON Zia's face was enough to make Cristhian smile. Genuinely. It was important she think love was an option if he was going to force that eventuality. It was imperative she thought *him* open to such things.

"Cristhian," she finally managed to say. "You… You can't be serious." But she sounded more…frightened than censuring. Interesting.

"The way I see it, we entered into this as strangers who shared an uncommon amount of chemistry. Hence the children."

She wrinkled her nose. "Yes, hence."

"Perhaps you did not go about it the way you should have, but we can set this aside."

"Oh. *Can* we?"

Again, his smile was genuine. She was entertaining at times, he'd give her that. "It is my understanding that the way people go about falling in love is to get to know each other. We should do this. See if we can't…open ourselves up to something."

She blinked once, as if she was trying to rid herself of the look of horror on her face. It didn't work.

He managed, just barely, not to laugh. "My parents

loved each other very much. My father's parents are the same."

"My guess is they did not meet in a bar and have a one-night stand that ended with twins."

"Perhaps not, but my parents met at a party and, by all accounts, were inseparable from that moment. My father's parents were far more scandalous. She was dating his best friend when they met at a church function, and she ditched one man for another." He shook his head.

She tried not to smile. He watched her fight it. But slowly the edges of her mouth curved.

"You love them very much."

He did not care for her having that insight, but it was only the truth. "They are good people. They never cared about titles or money. Their lives are simple—they complain when I try to make it simpler. Because they love their family, not what a person in it might offer them."

She sighed and settled deeper into her chair, studying a piece of fruit before setting it aside. "I love my sister. I've put her in an impossible situation with this, and…" She shook her head and spoke no more on it. Clearly it bothered her deeply.

But clearly she had still put herself over her sister's needs. A pattern for the princess.

He couldn't let his disdain for that show. Disdain did not grow love. Nor did suspicion, and she was clearly still suspicious of him. How did he combat that? It frustrated him that it would take time. Trust did not blossom overnight even in the easiest of situations.

"You say your parents loved each other," she said, picking at the hem on the sweater she wore. "But you were so young when they died." She chewed on her generous bottom lip for a moment before raising her gaze to meet his. "So how do you know they did?"

There was something vulnerable in the question, in her eyes, and it twisted something inside him, a strange need to protect that flash of something soft underneath all her strength and determination.

All her selfishness, he reminded himself. Because that was the issue with her, and he would not let her beauty, or even the odd flash of vulnerability, distract him from that.

He focused on her question and whether he would offer an answer. He did not often speak of his parents with anyone outside of his grandparents. It had been a topic he refused to engage with when it came to his mother's family, when it came to the odd reporter who still thought his life might make a story, or the random person he encountered who had known his parents.

Zia fit into none of those categories. He could make up a few lies, but trust was not built on outright lies, and worse, he never could quite bring himself to *lie* about his parents. It felt like betrayal.

"It was told to me, of course, how much they loved each other, as I grew up. Both as a positive from my father's parents, and a negative from my mother's family. But…children pick up more than adults think, I believe. Perhaps I did not have the maturity for the words yet, but there were things I witnessed that, looking back, could only have been love."

"Like what?" She looked truly intrigued, and he supposed there was no harm in this. It led her exactly where he wanted her, didn't it? Thinking about love, believing it could happen. And if he shared *his* definition of love, and tried to embody it, she would at least think him in love with her.

"I recall my father turning down roles that did not fit into her royal schedule. He would always laugh it off when the movies he turned down did well. He never made it seem…like a bad thing. It was always clear his family was the most important. Being with *her* was his goal. Movie stardom was almost more like…a hobby."

Cristhian frowned at his own words, and the feelings they dredged up. He had not thought of that in some time. The simple and easy ways his father had made Cristhian and his mother feel like the center of his world. He hadn't fully understood it as a child. But now, a man with a career and adult responsibilities, and the prospect of two children greeting him in a short period of time… It felt all that much more important.

Rare.

He dared not look at Zia with these strange feelings rioting around inside him. That would no doubt confuse things when his goals were clear. Even if the methods were murky.

"To my mother, he and I were the center of her world. Everything else a distraction. She struggled more with the lines there, what with the royal responsibilities her family wanted from her and how much her family disliked my father. But she made it clear time with my father was her goal as well."

So, in the here and now, Cristhian would make sure he made time for Zia. For the upcoming children. She would now take this as a sign of love, or potential love, and he would come out on top.

"I know my father does not love my mother," Zia said,

very, very quietly. "I highly doubt he ever did. She was a means to an end. His parents died when he was quite young, and he ascended. He needed a wife. A wife with the right pedigree to become a queen."

"This is often the way of royalty."

"Yes," she agreed. She sighed heavily. "But sometimes, I think she must love him to behave the way she does. Even if he does not love her, though I cannot fathom why he doesn't when she is everything he asks her to be."

"What way does she behave?" Cristhian asked before he thought better of it. Before he weighed what the answer would mean for his goals of getting Zia to fall in love with him.

"Afraid, I think. Oftentimes she will express agreement with me or my sister. She will act as though she will support us in the face of opposition—my father, his advisers and aides, and then the time comes and she… doesn't. She cowers."

Cristhian had seen an array of royal marriages in his adolescence, but he hadn't seen one like that. He supposed his uncle, the prince to his aunt's queen, had a kind of…cowering air about him. But it had never struck Cristhian as *fearful*.

But he understood that fear better than he liked. Because his mother's family had spent those first few years without his parents making things as scary as possible for a young boy. No stability. No support. He had been made to be afraid by people who only knew how to wield their power that way.

He felt an old anger simmer deep in his gut. There would not be *fear* in his children's lives. "Are you afraid of your father?" he asked Zia, trying to keep the old anger out of his tone.

She considered this, as if it required consideration. He did not like to see that kind of behavior continued or rewarded, and it *was* his business, he told himself. Because how Zia's parents dealt with her would inform how they dealt with *his* children, and he would not allow fear.

"I have never been afraid of him, no, because the things he cared about were not the things I cared about. But…with this pregnancy, I do have concerns about the reach of his power and what it could accomplish if I do not have full autonomy from it. He will consider these children his, in a way. Heirs."

Heirs. How Cristhian had come to hate that term in his life.

"Either way," Zia continued, "his family has never come above his country," Zia said firmly, as if fear did not matter. "I suppose that is the way of a king, and I shouldn't blame him for it." She shook her head as if to shake the words away. "Why are we discussing all this?"

"To get to know each other."

She studied him. "Because all of a sudden you think we could fall in love and somehow make a marriage work in a way that would support a family?"

"I realized it would be shortsighted not to be open to the idea, Zia."

He knew he'd gotten her there because she had no quick quip of a response. She just watched him with a thoughtful look on her face. Which was a good place to end things for this morning.

He rose from his chair, crossed to her. "I have a few

phone meetings I must attend to. I would like it if we could have tea together this afternoon."

"Oh. Well, I don't have anything better to do, I guess."

"Such a ringing endorsement, Princesa."

Her mouth twitched at the corner. "You're going to have to help me out of this chair, or I'm going to be stuck here until teatime."

He offered a hand and helped her up and out of the large chair. He did not release her, convinced this was the way toward getting what he wanted.

That was the *only* reason he lifted her hand to his mouth. The only possible impetus for brushing his mouth across her knuckles and watching the faint flush creep up her cheeks.

If he remembered all too well the way he'd made that flush take over her whole body months ago, there was nothing wrong with that. This was all part of his grand pursuit for her love.

That was all.

Zia had gone back to the conservatory for the next few hours. She had not been able to stop herself from dwelling on that strange morning. From his honest answers to hers. From the way her body still reacted to every last thing about him.

Was love really such a crazy idea? When her heart hammered about in her chest just from the way his gaze held hers, his lips barely touching her *hand*.

Love. She didn't really have a clue what love was. She loved her sister, her children-to-be. But that felt elemental. Just immediately and easily part of her. Not something that happened, but something that was.

Nothing about Cristhian felt that simple, that certain. It felt all jumbled and confusing—had before she'd even realized she was pregnant. Because no one had ever made her feel like that, and even when she'd walked away from him that morning all those months ago, she had believed nothing and no one would ever make her feel that way again.

It had been a sort of poetic, really. That *one* night.

Now a million nights stretched out before them with consequences complicating things, and that confused everything.

Even the stories he told of his parents and grandparents loving each other made it sound like love was some immediate thing. She had felt attraction for Cristhian, lust, certainly, and everything she learned about him was interesting.

Were those ingredients to love?

And if they were, was that even something she wanted to consider? It seemed a dangerous element to add between them when they had to put their children first and foremost. Not each other. How could she take care of her children if she was worried about taking care of him?

She ruminated over that for the next few hours. She'd been brought lunch up in the conservatory. She'd enjoyed the plants, read a little, dozed. She'd even risked a text to Beau. Still just to assure her sister things were fine, not to ask for help…yet.

They were stuck in this castle for a few days. Perhaps she should simply…hear Cristhian out. Get to know him. She didn't know how to believe in something like love as some magical answer to this complicated problem, but maybe understanding could lead to…

She blew out a breath, frustrated with her mind turning in the same circles. Because it always came back to the fact that everything she understood about relationships was that one person inevitably came out the victor.

Even with Beau, whom she loved with her whole heart, everything ended up a contest with a winner and a loser. And she always tried to protect Beau from being the loser. A protection born out of necessity—the heir, the...very much not heir.

And now you've left Beau with all that baggage. So who's the victor?

"Ugh," she said aloud, to try to force herself out of the loop. She couldn't fix what was going on at home, whatever Beau was dealing with, though Beau insisted she was fine.

But Zia could find a way to deal with her current situation. Cristhian. These babies. She had to. That was her responsibility now.

She spent a considerable amount of time having to maneuver herself out of the chair and onto her feet. Sometimes, she had the fleeting thought that she would be quite glad when she wasn't pregnant any longer.

Then she thought about the fact that two babies had to come *out* of her, and she walked that back pretty fast. And did something to forget about the very looming realities creeping up on her.

She went in search of Cristhian since it was nearing their agreed-upon teatime. She hoped there were more pastries. She hadn't been exaggerating about his cook. He was a miracle worker with sugar and butter.

Lucky for her.

She didn't make it all the way downstairs before she

ran into Cristhian. He was standing on a landing on the grand staircase, looking out one of the tall, narrow windows. Outside, there were no longer rolls of white. It was just…all white. She couldn't discern anything beyond snow.

More snow. A blizzard.

He glanced at her. "I was on my way to fetch you." He nodded toward the window. "We may be stuck a few more days yet."

She rubbed at her stomach, trying not to worry. "I have an appointment with my doctor in three days."

"My doctor is on his way. This might set her back another day or two, but it should not be impossible to get her here in that time frame." He turned to face her fully now, standing a few stairs above him. He studied her. "Do you have concerns we need taken care of?"

Zia shook her head. "No. So far everything has been right on track. Twins offer more risk, but I have not displayed any risk factors."

"I have not asked. When are they due?"

"My doctor was hoping I would make it to thirty-six weeks without needing any interventions to extend the pregnancy. I will be at thirty-four weeks at my next appointment. So far, so good. A full term would be another six weeks, but that's unlikely. Next month, probably."

Cristhian nodded at this information. Then he offered his arm. "Tea is set up in the dining room."

She hesitated. No matter how she felt about him on an intellectual level, even something as platonic as linking her arm with his was dangerous. He was too…*something*. Even when she wanted to hate him, every touch was charged with electricity. Like he was a current she would always react to.

But something too close to smug appeared on the lines of his face, like he understood her reluctance, so she straightened her shoulders and took the last few stairs to link arms with his.

And it *was* electric, no matter how stiffly she held herself against it. The heat of him, that spicy scent that had haunted her dreams these past few months. No doubt some cologne he wore, but also just *him*.

"Tell me more about your sister," he offered conversationally as they walked down the rest of the staircase.

"Why?"

He shrugged. "I am curious. I have no siblings, and we are to have twins. What is that like?"

"Well, it's hard to explain, since I don't know what it's *not* like. In some ways, it was a great gift to always have Beaugonia by my side."

"And in others?"

"When you are a twin, it is a constant comparison. Who is developing faster? Who has a higher intellect? Which one's prettier? Which one's more rebellious?"

"And yet you speak of her as if you are not in competition."

Zia shook her head as he led her into the dining room. Another cornucopia of delightful-looking food—small sandwiches, more pastries, desserts. He certainly knew how to feed a woman if nothing else. "Those were outside forces. Our parents, royal staff, media. *I* never felt in competition to Beau."

"Did she you?"

He helped her into her seat as she considered the question. "I don't think so. Beau is…unique. She has always been more…interior than I am. The outside world doesn't often factor into her decision-making. She has never expressed to me any real competition, but that is the thing about twins. It doesn't matter what the two of you do, the outside world will judge you against each other all the same."

"And so you were chosen as heir. Because, in comparison, you came out on top?"

"Because I could be told what to do," she corrected. It had taken her until just a few years ago to realize this. That it wasn't just luck of the draw that people saw her as more suitable. Maturity had made her realize it was her ability to be manipulated that led her into the life of heir.

But she didn't want him to think that was still the case. As much as she didn't want to let him into every facet of her life, he needed to understand that obedience and ability to be manipulated had been bred into her.

She didn't fall for it anymore. Only when she needed to protect Beau. "I think I was only twelve or thirteen when they informed me of the trajectory of my life. Marry a royal my father would choose. Produce many a child with said royal so that, since I would be acting queen of whatever husband's country, one of my children could be heir to my father's throne *and* this other throne. And so, last year, the crown prince was chosen, and I was told I would marry him. Our countries would be linked in a positive way for both. A familiar pressure was pushed upon me to agree, and I caved to it."

"You speak of an obedience I have yet to see considering both times we have met, you have been running away."

She shook her head. "When I first met you, it wasn't to run away. I had given myself a week to…escape. Briefly. I had a time limit. I just wanted to see what it would be like to make my own decisions, have my own life. I thought it would help. Obviously, I was a bit naive there, and then compounded that naivete with a mistake with you. But at the end of the day, my father had made it very clear to me if I did not do *my* duty, that Beau's life would suffer. So I was going to do my duty."

She poured the tea while he filled both their plates. Small domestic movements that felt strangely…comforting. She supposed because they were stuck here, in this unreal world, where they could get along and nothing outside the walls of the castle had to matter.

But this was very temporary, and she needed to remember that.

"It seems to me your sister is a grown woman who can handle herself if she is as you describe. Why are you so protective?"

"In some ways she is that." She would not let Cristhian or anyone else in on Beau's issues. Not because she felt as her parents did that Beau's panic attacks were embarrassing and a bad mark on the crown. If anything, she felt the opposite. Beau's issues meant she deserved protecting from *anyone*.

Silence fell after that, as if he expected her to fill it. She didn't. She busied herself with baked goods and tea. When he finally spoke again, it seemed he'd realized she wouldn't speak any more about her sister.

"And what did you do on this week of freedom you took? Besides me, of course."

She laughed in spite of herself. Perhaps she was giving

him too much information, too much ammunition. But maybe…maybe she could allow him to fall in love with her, if she believed such things possible. As long as *she* didn't fall in love, didn't have to serve him in that way, that meant she had control of the situation.

Didn't it?

"I shopped alone," she said, thinking back to that glorious week. So glorious she'd let everything go wrong, and even now, couldn't regret it. "I went to a concert and lost myself in the music *I* chose to like. I walked in cities at night, in broad daylight, all on my own. I even found an athletic club and joined a little pickup football game one day. No one treated me any different than anyone else. It was like breathing for the first time."

He didn't say anything right away. He was staring at her intently, an odd expression on his face she couldn't quite parse. Intense, yes, but as if he was trying to puzzle her out, like she was some sort of brain teaser.

"Were you expecting something else?" she asked.

He shook his head, looked down at his plate. "I do not know what I expected."

But he got that look about him. She was beginning to recognize it was usually when he brought up something about royalty. And his mother was a princess. Like her.

"Did your mother ever try to step out of royal life?"

His expression shuttered. "I should like to meet your sister, I think. Perhaps we can get her here for the wedding."

She did not know if he meant to be provoking, or if he was simply so used to always telling people how it would be that he did not consider her feelings on the wedding she hadn't agreed to at all.

"I haven't agreed to marry you, Cristhian," she stated very firmly.

He looked over at her and smiled then, and she should *not* react to that. It shouldn't flutter through her like some heady liquor. He was smiling because he thought what she wanted didn't matter.

And still she throbbed with too many memories of *that* night to name.

"My mistake, Princesa," he said, his voice a low, sultry menace. "More tea?"

CHAPTER TEN

CRISTHIAN FELT AS though he were making some progress. Zia was forthcoming with most information. About her family, her upbringing, what she wanted for the children.

She was a fascinating woman. She had a wide variety of interests, and she talked easily and happily about most of them. When he prodded about her family in an effort to determine the best way to handle them, she presented a strange figure. Obedient, yet driven by an internal need to be herself. Easily manipulated by an authoritarian father, and yet not ignorant or foolish. Most of her purpose, at least as she stated it, was to protect her sister.

If he felt like there were some similarities there, in how she viewed the royal machine in many of the same ways he did, well... He didn't think too deeply on it. Similarities didn't mean anything. Not when he had a situation to control in order to ensure the best outcomes for everyone.

He had not yet figured out how she could talk of her sister so protectively, and yet have abandoned the woman to handle the mess Zia herself had made. He could not quite make sense of the spoiled princess who clearly did as she pleased, and yet, at times, had not. And the more he dug into these seemingly disparate facets of her, the more she took up residence in his mind even when he was not spending time with her.

He was quite sure he could have handled all this, even if it was a tad alarming and unique, if it weren't for the physical undercurrents that still traveled between them.

He knew she was attracted to him still. She could not hide her reaction to him. The issue was that he had his own reaction to her, and he did not care for it. She haunted his dreams, in that same way she had before he'd known she carried his children. As if this huge turn of events had not changed anything at all.

When it *should*.

Still, Cristhian had not lost his head. He had continued to engage her in conversation, in meals together. He had worked on charming her, and he thought he was succeeding as that suspicious look rarely crossed her face anymore. He would have been happy to leave it at just the two of them for a few days more yet, but he could sense she had some concerns about her doctor's appointment, so he had done everything in his considerable power to have the doctor arrive, hiring an entire fleet of people to get the doctor across closed roads and looming snowdrifts.

Though he still felt marriage the best course of action, and certainly something that needed to be acted upon before they approached any signs of her going into labor, making certain all three parties were healthy was paramount to everything else.

Even worrying about getting a clergy member who could marry them to the castle.

The doctor arrived one snowy afternoon, with the fleet he'd hired to get her to the castle safely.

She was a middle-aged woman with a no-nonsense way about her that Cristhian appreciated, and her reputation was one of excellent work and, just as important, working with royals and celebrities and never once letting their secrets wind their way into the press.

Cristhian still had not contacted King Rendall, and since the king's own men had searched for months for Zia with no luck, he figured he still had a few weeks yet before he needed to answer to the man.

He would do so with a clear way forward. This respite wasn't *running away*. It was preparing a battle plan. Just as he had done once as a young man, ready to cut ties with his mother's family. More or less.

"I can do an exam," the doctor explained to him as they walked up the staircase to Zia's room. "But a paternity test will have to wait until we have access to a lab without worrying about the state of the roads."

Cristhian nodded. He had not been lying to Zia about not having any true concerns about paternity, but a child of his, a child of hers… There would need to be legal proof along with protection. So that would be the next step after this.

When they knocked on the door to her suite, Zia answered the door herself. He made the introductions, there was some brief small talk, and then the doctor got to work. She didn't seem to have much in the way of equipment, but she chatted cheerfully while she worked, setting Zia up in her bed, propped up on pillows.

She took vitals, then talked them through the process, explaining her sonogram machine—an incredibly small little device—would transmit the images to her laptop screen, set up on the nightstand next to the doctor. Cristhian was somewhat dubious of the equipment, but once she started…he forgot all about technology.

On the screen, it was black and gray. The gray and white forming different shapes against the black. The doctor held her little machine this way and that on Zia's round stomach. She made considering noises, but Cristhian couldn't begin to imagine what they meant.

Then it was hard to listen to her, because she explained the odd *womp-womp* noise that filled the room was a heartbeat. And then another.

His children's hearts. Beating. The sound echoed inside him like some kind of avalanche.

Eventually, the doctor took the machine off Zia's stomach, and gave Zia permission to get comfortable. She clicked a few keys on her laptop and pulled up one of the sonogram images.

"This is Baby A," she explained, and she outlined the head, an arm, a knee. She did the same with Baby B. She mentioned heart rates and growth patterns, but Cristhian couldn't take it all in once he could fully recognize what she outlined as bodies.

He had seen the physical evidence of them all these days from the size of Zia's stomach. He had been fascinated that two children could be nestled inside her, and still…this was something else entirely.

Hearts beating. Limbs moving. Life. A life he'd had a hand in creating. It swamped him, in a way perhaps he had not allowed himself to fully accept yet.

"You are very lucky, ma'am," the doctor said to Zia. "Everything is just as it should be. I see no risk factors for preterm labor. At this rate, you could make it to thirty-six weeks and perhaps even after. We'll want to keep a close eye on things, of course, but everything is just as it should be."

But Zia wasn't looking at the doctor, and neither was he.

"We can discuss the sex, if you'd like," the doctor continued.

Neither of them looked at the doctor. Neither of them answered her. The doctor cleared her throat, but Cristhian could not take his eyes off the tears in Zia's. The way everything about her shone with some... He did not know. He felt bowled over by *everything*. Like he was no longer the foundation he stood on, survived on.

Like something else had upended him, wrestled his control and strength away. Which was ludicrous, of course, and a thought to be pushed away. Without control, only danger and tragedy lay ahead.

"I'll...give you two a private moment," the doctor said. "Then we can discuss next steps once you're ready."

Cristhian had no idea if the doctor left then. He couldn't have cared less. He couldn't seem to break his gaze from the myriad of Zia's green. The tears that spilled over now, dotting her cheeks like sparkling jewels.

He brushed the tears away. "What is this?" he murmured, something heavy and painful in his chest, and yet it held no candle to the pain the tears brought.

Zia shook her head and sniffled. "I cry every time I hear their heartbeats. Not out of any sadness. It's just so amazing. I don't know how to explain it. They just...are about to exist in this world and I..." Her voice squeaked, and she made a vague kind of gesture.

But she didn't have to explain what she felt. Perhaps he would not shed any tears, but he understood the *over-*

whelmingness. It was just…too big, this reality of theirs. Children. *Children*. Coming sooner rather than later. Each their own individual person who would exist and live in this world.

So he took Zia's hand in his, sat next to her on the bed. Trying to find some semblance of the anchor that had once tethered him to earth.

She made a little "oh" noise, then her mouth curved. She squeezed his hand and pulled it to her stomach. She pressed his palm there, right at the side of the swell of their children.

"Do you feel it?" she asked.

But he did not know what he was meant to feel, and not knowing left him perfectly speechless.

He always knew.

Her mouth curved, even with the evidence of the tears still on her cheeks, as though she understood he was at a complete and utter loss. Unacceptable.

But before he could do anything about that, wrestle control of the situation back in place, she pressed his hand into her stomach with more force, and then he felt it…something *ripple* across his hand. If he had been un-tethered before, this became the anchor to everything.

His child, moving, there underneath her skin. This new version of his life. A new reason for *everything*. A purpose born of the future rather than the past.

And it all centered on Zia. Not just because she carried these babies, but because she was the mitigating factor. She was…

He did not know. Found he did not want to delve too much into these thoughts scrambling around in his mind, only half formed. So he pushed them out of his mind the only way he knew how.

He pressed his mouth to hers. Like he had those months ago. As if he was finding some new answer to an old question. Perhaps she *was* the answer.

Because she kissed him back. Like the moment had bowled her over, too. Rearranged something inside her, when she'd had all these months to carry this new life and grow it inside her and become accustomed to it all.

Everything had changed and yet she tasted the same. A same he shouldn't remember quite as well as he did. Still, for all that *same*, she was different under his hands. Ripe and round and lovely. She sighed into him, like she had found respite after a long journey and this intoxicating feeling was new, strange, heady.

Her arms came around him. All the heat and flame they'd been ignoring for these past few days lighting between them.

Not smart, when he was always smart. Not in control, when he was always in control.

Except when it came to her.

Zia felt as though she were drowning in a storm of too many things. Joy. Fear. Hope and anxiety. Need, want, lust.

And the impossible and irresistible chemistry between them. She had been so sure she could resist it. Avoid it. That his sudden and unwanted appearance in her life, complete with overbearing decisions and control issues, *clearly*, should have taken all of this away.

But no.

It was not as though she had gone about kissing many

a man. She'd had her little rebellions, just to prove to her father that he would not have a say in *everything* she did, even if he had a say in the last things she did.

But nothing had ever remotely felt like this. Like she might die if she did not get to experience that night again.

Just once, she thought to herself. It was the heat of the moment. Zia tried to assure herself of this. She just… hadn't had anyone with her for any of these checkups. It was just the emotion that always struck her, but she had someone to pour it into.

But he was different, and she knew it. No matter how little she liked it.

The way he kissed her was like altering all the shaky foundations she'd managed to build since she'd left his bed, since she'd found out she was pregnant, and then that there were *two* babies. She had lovingly placed every floorboard in this brand-new life.

And he'd taken an axe to all of them. Hacked it all to pieces.

In the flame of this kiss she didn't care. Who needed foundations when she had his arms around her and his mouth on her? When his hands smoothed over her stomach as if he sought to protect the little lives she grew?

And then lower, to stoke every fire that had ever existed within her, like they existed just for him.

She wanted him. Again. Even knowing it was a mistake. A temporary madness, really. But who cared in this temporary moment, knowing how good it would feel?

One of the babies rolled, long and hard against her stomach. Against *him*. He startled, pulling back and staring at her stomach in a kind of shock that made her want to laugh.

Not *at* him. Just at everything. And this strange, dizzying joy that came with it all, when she should know better than to believe in someone, in something. But no matter how hard she tried in this life to remind herself everyone else was living in a competition even if she didn't realize it, she didn't want to feel she was at war with *him*.

So when their gazes met, she was smiling in spite of herself. His gaze was hot, fervent. But he did not press his mouth to her again. Carefully, gingerly almost, he released her and got up off the bed. "The doctor is waiting." He said this as though he had some control, but she watched the way he struggled to catch his breath. She saw the wild need in his eyes that couldn't quite leave hers.

But if he could find some kernel of control in all this, so could she. "Yes." The doctor. Sonograms and babies and…all that entailed. She could be in control, too. She could…be just as strong as him. The doctor was waiting because she had more information to impart.

Zia steeled herself to meet his dark, intense gaze. "Would you like to know the sex?" she managed to ask, though her voice sounded a bit strangled.

He didn't say anything at first. He kept staring at her with all that *fire* that had her curling her hands into fists so she did not reach for him.

"I would, yes, if that is acceptable to you." His voice was a rasp, reminding her of too many pieces of that night she'd spent with him. His mouth, his hands, the things he made her feel with just that dark, delicious voice of his.

But this was not that night. So she managed a tiny

nod even though it wasn't a question exactly. Still, she thought, maybe with someone by her side, she *was* ready. Or maybe it was just that time was running out, and she had to be ready whether she liked it or not.

He strode out of the bedroom, and within a few minutes was back with the doctor. Whose gaze moved from Cristhian to Zia in a way that had Zia blushing.

Profusely.

"Mr. Sterling has informed me you'd like to know the sex now."

Zia nodded.

"A boy," the doctor said. "And a girl. The girl is currently measuring a bit smaller than baby boy, but this is very common with twins, and so far, not a concern."

A boy. A girl. Zia didn't know why this came as such a shock. She supposed that because she had a twin sister, she'd just…always imagined them both as girls. Even *knowing* they could be one or two boys, she hadn't been able to visualize that.

Now, with their father standing next to her, she could visualize far too many things. Children with darker features. One that looked like her, and one like him.

This made her want to cry all over again.

"Mr. Sterling? If you'll excuse us? I'd like to have a private discussion with the expectant mother."

Cristhian frowned at the doctor, but then he looked at Zia and some strange emotion she couldn't parse passed over his face. He nodded. "Very well." He gave Zia one last confusing look, and then turned and left the bedroom.

Zia had to force herself to tear her gaze from the door

and smile politely at the doctor. "Thank you for braving the roads and such. It has put my mind at ease."

"I'm glad. These last weeks of pregnancy can be stressful, but rest assured, you will be well taken care of. As a physician, I want it to be clear. While I will be staying here throughout the rest of your term, per Mr. Sterling's request, and with his compensation, my duty is to you, ma'am. Your health, and your children's health. You can come to me with any questions, voice any opinion you like. And I will always be honest with my recommendations."

Zia blinked at the woman. While these were all nice things to hear, she supposed she hadn't thought that far ahead. Hadn't considered that Cristhian might hire a doctor who *wouldn't* put her health first.

What a terrible thought. But the doctor kept talking.

"I have worked with many…well-known individuals. The rich and powerful. My record is above reproach. Never once have I been the source of gossip. Nor have I ever let a powerful man have sway over someone's health."

"This is all very comforting to hear, of course," Zia said carefully. "But I… I guess I don't know where it's coming from."

"Intercourse is not off the table," the doctor said matter-of-factly.

Zia nearly choked on nothing but her own saliva. "I'm sorry?"

"You'll want to monitor how you feel. If there's any cramping, bleeding, discomfort after, you would want to avoid it from there on out."

Zia could not stop the hot blush that worked up her

cheeks. She had to clear her throat to speak as she wrapped her arms around her stomach. "I wouldn't want to put them at risk."

The doctor shrugged as if this was a very normal conversation, and she supposed it was. For parents who were married or in a relationship. It *was* straightforward for those people, no doubt.

But nothing was straightforward for her and Cristhian. No matter what the doctor said about it.

"We always want a mother to come as close to term as possible, particularly with twins," she said, as though delivering a well-practiced speech. "But you are very healthy, your babies are very healthy. The risks are minimal at this stage. That can always change, but it might not. You have your own wants and needs, ma'am. Those are valid, too. But not a requirement of you, either."

It all made a weird kind of sense now. The doctor was making sure she understood the green light was not because Cristhian was paying her, but because it was a perfectly reasonable option. But she left the caveat in, because no doubt women had been in her position where they had *not* wanted to deal with the advances of the men who were overseeing their health.

"I'm at your service, whenever you need," the doctor said.

Zia managed a nod. "Thank you. I appreciate it. Genuinely."

"I'll leave you then, unless you have more questions?"

Zia shook her head. No. Not questions. Uncertainty, yes. But not questions. The doctor left her alone with her whirling thoughts. She pushed herself up and out of the bed and walked over to one of the windows, looking out into all that white.

The snow had stopped falling again, but still so much had piled up around the castle. It still felt like a fairy-tale world she knew she could not let herself be fooled by.

But she *wanted* to be. Just another day or two. Fooled and foolish. Believing in fairy tales of happily-ever-afters instead of the harsh reality of responsibility and control and protecting those she loved in whatever ways she could.

Beau. Her babies.

End of list.

Cristhian stepped into the bedroom then. He closed the door behind him. And Zia knew there was still a choice to be had here. She did not *have* to give in to her body's desires. She could use her brain, protect her heart that felt so strangely bruised after all of this.

But she didn't.

CHAPTER ELEVEN

ZIA STOOD JUST out of reach, looking like some beautiful statue. A paragon of fertility and female beauty. Regal. Knowing. The light from outside shining on her like some kind of beacon.

For a moment, just a flash, Cristhian could picture himself on his knees worshipping at her very feet.

The problem with love, mi princesa, *is that it is beyond our control. And we are beyond theirs.*

Sometimes he preferred to think of memories as dreams, rather than flashes of his childhood.

But that voice in his head was his father's—American accent and all—and the image of his parents together, while she cried over some royal slight, was real. Stuck in his head. Because once his father had seen him there, he'd beckoned him over. Insisted they go on a picnic. And his mother had stopped crying. They had enjoyed a perfect afternoon.

That happy memory, of that picnic, of his father's love, was the reason he felt this way. It had nothing to do with *her.* He wouldn't allow it. Things were too complicated already.

Weren't they?

Cristhian took a step back before what he realized he

was doing. *Retreat? Never.* He lifted his chin, continued to study her. But this did not help. She was some beautiful siren, luring him off course.

"I liked her," Zia said at last. "You made an excellent choice."

"I am glad. She will remain on property until the children are born."

Something flitted through her expression he did not quite recognize, but she put one hand over her stomach in a protective gesture, as if she was afraid of…something.

A sharp, curling need took him over then. It was the only way to explain it. He moved toward her. "You will have the best of everything, Zia." He touched her shoulder, couldn't seem to stop himself, even though he had never been any good at comfort. But he had to do something to assuage that fear. "There is nothing to worry about."

She huffed out a little laugh. "Only a man could say that. There is *so* much to worry about." Still, she put her hand over his on her shoulder and smiled up at him. "But I appreciate the… I know we want the same thing. Two happy, healthy babies."

"Yes." But it felt like she was leaving something out.

He didn't want to think at all about what it might be. Because his children would come first. Before his own happiness. And hers. He would organize their lives so that everything turned out better than his had.

It put them at a crossroads, because he knew she put herself first. She had made that clear to him, and he would not let her do that to his children. His children would never know this conflict between them, though. Cristhian would ensure it.

He wanted Zia, yes. With a need that was blinding him to what was necessary. What was right. Such was her power, but he was a man in control of himself. In control of *everything*.

He could leave.

He *would* leave.

But her hand was on his. Her body so close. That lush mouth of hers tilted up, just within reach. A taste… What was a little taste? It would just keep her thinking love was an option.

Perhaps she would even mistake it for love. He could kiss her and maintain control. Because if she loved him, that would be all the control he needed.

Warning bells sounded in his head. The kind he listened to in his work. Those gut feelings he never took for granted. Because so often they told him where he was making a misstep, warned him he was going down a wrong path.

Today, he ignored them and pressed his mouth to hers. Just another small taste. Not for him, but to fool her. *Her*.

She met his kiss, pressed her palms to his cheeks as she lifted to her toes to get a better angle. Sweet and lovely, with enough bite to send a jolt through his system.

Control. I am in control.

He was sure of it.

"The doctor said it was safe," she whispered against his mouth. He looked down at her, and those siren-green eyes, a myriad of colors he was drowning in.

Because it was a simple sentence, but her expression showed a variety of complexity behind that it.

Safe. Not just safe, but here Zia stood giving him the go-ahead. When it was not *safe* for either of them. It was just like that first and only night. A loss of control. No doubt full of consequences that would echo through them forever.

He knew what consequences did. He knew what happened when he gave up his control.

He kissed her anyway. Deep and hard, pouring months and months of frustration into her. Because how he had *dreamed* of her against his will. How he had *wanted* her and been unable to want anyone or anything else.

She had ruined him somehow, and this felt like control. Like reclaiming…something. So he claimed her mouth. He lifted her shirt off her and let it fall to the ground, claiming her breasts, the stomach where she carried their children.

So perfect, lush and vibrant. He remembered with a ferocity it didn't do to dwell on every inch of her, but she had changed. Become fuller, softer. So he cataloged this new version of her, laying her out on the bed, naked and perfect just for him. He studied her, with his hands, with his mouth. Until she was all but sobbing out his name, writhing there on this large bed.

His. *His*. Because together they created something bigger than themselves. Not just the result of their night together, but this all-encompassing thing that stripped him of his control, his certainty. Stripped him of everything he was.

Because in this moment all he could be was *hers*.

He stripped himself of his own clothes, slid his palms along her inner thighs, opening her for him. He slid into her in one long, slow stroke, the wave of pleasure and *right* sweeping through him like an eruption. As if things had not been right since she'd left his bed that morning, and now they finally could be again.

She cried out, shuddering around him almost immediately. So responsive, always, like they had been designed to bring out a pleasure in each other that no one else could even begin to know.

So he moved, slow and steady, drawing her up that heady peak once more. Watching as the pleasure chased over her gorgeous features. He watched her mouth form his name, and he felt her lose herself once more around him.

He roared out his own release as she held on to him, strong and sure. But it left him feeling none of those things. Fear sneaked in under all the swirling pleasure as she rolled into him, as he pulled her close.

He held her too tight, he knew. This was out of his control. Beyond his rules. He had crossed all his own lines, and he had to get them back into place. The only way to take hold of this situation was to make certain everything happened the way he saw fit.

"You will marry me, Zia."

He shouldn't have said it. He didn't know what had come over him. Just a need to have everything right and in place and her to be…

Mine.

But not that. Not in *that* way. Just in the way that… that they would… That would allow him to make everything right. Make the *world* right.

For his children. That was all.

Zia was amazed that someone could ruin something so thoroughly and so quickly. For a moment, the pleasure and joy of finding what they had had their first night had completely taken her over. There'd been some sliver of hope that something…good and right could come out of all of this.

Then he'd crushed it. While the orgasm still pulsed through her. She wriggled away from his too-tight grip, from that fervent, nearly wild gaze.

Maybe later she could consider what that lack of control on his face meant. Maybe later she could give him some benefit of the doubt. But in the here and now? The only way to protect herself was to lash out.

"So, that's not a question," she said, searching the floor for her clothes. When she couldn't find them, she jerked a blanket off the bed and wrapped it around her.

He made a sound perilously close to a growl. "It is the appropriate course of action."

"Have you been talking to my father? You sound just like him." Which was possibly only an insult in *her* mind. But one that showed her just how stupid she could be. Leave it to her to be so consumed by a man as obsessed with control as any king.

He pulled on his pants, somehow looking perfectly businesslike and in control while she no doubt looked like a ridiculous potato wrapped in his blanket.

He seared her with a look. "You cannot take me to your bed and oppose marriage."

"I think you'll find that not only *can* I, but I do."

"You are being contrary for the sake of it."

She shook her head, even though a little voice in her head whispered, *Aren't you?* But as contrary as she *could* be, this wasn't about anything like that. Because it wasn't about her. It was about their future, and how she could ensure it was the right one for their children.

"No, Cristhian. I will not go from one controlling ogre to another. I will have some say in my life, and so will my children."

"Our children."

"*Our* means we share. *Our* means there are two people involved. *Our* means you don't just get to…order things and have them be so. *Our* is a compromise."

He held his jaw so tight now it was a wonder he didn't crush his own teeth to dust. Anger simmered in his eyes, but when he spoke, he sounded very calm. Very cool.

"It is interesting that you feel qualified to give lectures on what *our* means, when everything you demonstrate is that you are only interested in *you*."

It shouldn't hurt. She shouldn't let him fool her into thinking they were more than strangers. A few days of meals and conversations didn't mean you knew someone well enough to…

It didn't matter. Whatever she thought or didn't, he clearly saw her as someone too selfish to understand an *our*. "Is that what you think of me?" she asked, trying to use his calm, cool tone.

He did not answer right away. He stared at her, his entire body seemingly taut like it was ready to explode. But he didn't do that, she'd give him some credit there.

"I was hoping that you would be willing to be reasonable," he said after a long, strained moment of silence.

"You were hoping that good sex would lead me to believe we were in love and should be married immediately." Which nearly made her want to cry. That he'd just been using it as a weapon, not this irresistible need she had felt it was. "What you fail to understand is that I already knew the sex was good, Cristhian. *That* is not the concern." She pointed at the rumpled bed. "This isn't some new experience that was about to change my mind about anything."

His expression went…arrested, almost. Like she'd stabbed him straight through and he was surprised to find it hurt. She didn't know what to think of that, or why it should make her feel small and hurting.

Then he smoothed it all out. Back to in-control, certain Cristhian Sterling who ruled the world. "I will contact your father immediately and inform him that you have been found, and we will be married."

It was absolutely ridiculous that she was shocked. *Hurt.* She knew better. But somehow…he'd fooled her. "What happened to the possibility of love?"

He eyed her, like she was some…piece of gum stuck to the bottom of his shoe, as if gum would dare. "I thought you could be reasonable. I thought, perhaps, there *was* a possibility that underneath the pampered princess veneer, there was a woman who could see beyond herself to the life she could give her children. Now that I see that I was wrong, we will proceed my way."

She was struggling to breathe normally, to keep the tears that wanted to fall in check. She would be strong. For those children he didn't think she cared about. Because she would not be a doormat. She would not *bend* for him. Because Zia knew, deep and personal, that a mother like that wasn't a good mother at all.

"I won't say yes."

"I won't need you to." And with that, he left her room

with quick, certain strides. So fast she couldn't even find the words to argue with him.

He couldn't *force* her to marry him. No matter what he said.

I will call your father.

What had happened? She sank onto the edge of the bed, at a total loss. How had sex turned into this…this? How had thinking they could find some common ground flipped so quickly?

What had she done so wrong?

She shook her head. No, she wouldn't blame herself. Well, not fully. She had made mistakes, yes. She had let her guard down, and then she had let something as foolish as chemistry cloud her good judgment.

Because it *was* good judgment to not want to jump into marriage. If they married, he would have all the say. Over her, over the children. There would be no compromise.

He could talk about love all he wanted, but she had nothing to offer him. No way to protect a man like him. How could he love what essentially was a useless object to him?

For the first time, she pictured those children. Cristhian ordering them the way her father had ordered her. She would stand up for them, of course, like her mother never had.

But in this new visualization, with actual children, with Cristhian, she almost thought she understood why her mother caved.

Because what was worse? The caving to avoid the explosion, or the explosions themselves? If she fought Cristhian in front of their children, was that really any better for them? She had never witnessed her mother put up a fight, and she'd always thought she wanted to.

But now…with her in the mother role, she wasn't so sure. That wouldn't feel safe to two little children. Angry parents, conflicting parents.

So how did she make this right?

She pulled out her phone with shaky hands.

Beau. I need help…

CHAPTER TWELVE

CRISTHIAN KEPT EXPECTING the fury to fade, but it didn't. It just…flipped. Because as angry as he was at the woman Zia was, the real, enduring anger was at himself.

He'd mishandled everything that day with the doctor. And then spent the next two days allowing her to ignore and avoid him while he arranged all the plans that he knew were right.

He didn't need her to agree to know they were right, and he was hardly going to scrape and beg to get her to see his way of things. Married parents, living together under the same roof: this was what his children deserved, and nothing could change that.

That was why he had used considerable money and influence to get all the roads from airport to castle cleared. That was why he'd flown in staff from his home base estate in Spain. That was why Zia's family was on their way to the cottage and would arrive at any moment.

Tomorrow, they were going to have a royal wedding. No matter *who* approved. Even his bride.

Once that was out of the way, a paternity test situated, they would bring in the lawyers. Everything would be carefully and *legally* outlined. So that neither the king nor his own so-called "family" would have a say in his children's lives.

They would be protected at all costs.

He had given this a lot of thought. More than Zia, clearly. Sure, she had escaped her father for a few months, but then King Rendall had hired *Cristhian* to find her, and while Cristhian might be the best and the most discreet about that sort of thing, there was likely someone else King Rendall could hire who would eventually track her down. And then what? Did she have *any* plans besides running away?

He thought of his parents and convinced himself he didn't know why they were on the forefront of his mind lately. It was simply because he was in the process of becoming a parent himself.

It wasn't about love. It wasn't about their own runaway attempt that had ended so horribly.

Because what Zia didn't understand was that running away would never be the answer. Being under his protection was the only way forward, and there was no point wasting any more time trying to win her over.

Cristhian didn't know why this felt different from his usual decisions. Why he woke up every morning with a strange tension inside him, fingers curled into fists, as if he was constantly fighting in his sleep.

He didn't know why whirling feelings and second thoughts plagued him when he had not allowed something so pointless since he'd been a teenager.

There were no second thoughts here. Control would keep everyone safe and sound.

He'd put his plan into action, so now everyone would

see it through. And no one would end up dying on the side of the road.

He pushed that thought away mercilessly. Because this was not about his parents. It was about his present.

He was standing in his office, looking out one of the large windows with a view of the rolling hills of his estate. All covered in a picturesque white, while flurries started again. A snow globe, a postcard, a fairy tale. But even when everything looked beautiful from the outside, it was still messy, uncertain life on the inside.

Which was why Cristhian had to put his stamp of control on what was happening.

When he was informed that the small royal motorcade had pulled up to the cottage, he left his office and went to greet his guests. The minister had been delayed a little, but Cristhian had been assured he would arrive later today.

Cristhian had decided to let Zia continue to hide in her room. She did not know that her parents were coming, he didn't think. Unless she'd had communication with her sister. Possible, but Cristhian did not concern himself with informing her of his plans.

She would be part of them whether she liked it or not, so there was no point having a conversation that would no doubt only end in more conflict.

He was done with conflict.

A staff member opened the large front door, while more staff ushered the royal family inside.

"Your Majesties. Your Highness." He gave a short bow to the three royals who stood on the threshold of his home. "Welcome."

He had not met the queen before, but he could see

bits and pieces of Zia in her. The green eyes, the sharp chin. Her expression was one of regal distance, but she gripped her husband's arm so tight the knuckles on her hand were white.

The younger woman who stood behind the king and queen, almost as if she was purposely trying to hide, was Zia's sister, no doubt. Zia's twin. For twins, they did not look too much alike. Sure, there was a sisterly resemblance in coloring, but he supposed he'd expected something more like imprints of each other. But where Zia was tall, athletic, regal, Beaugonia was smaller, softer. Her eyes were more hazel, but sharp and taking everything in, even as she kept herself as much out of the center as possible.

"I hope you traveled well. It's not a long journey, I know, but my staff can show you to your rooms if you'd like to rest up before dinner."

King Rendall looked down at him with a clearly growing suspicion. "I have come here as a courtesy since you claim to have found my daughter."

"I appreciate such courtesy," Cristhian replied with an easy smile. He gestured at his staff who were bringing in the royal family's belongings. "They will show you the way to your rooms."

"Where is my daughter?" the queen asked. King Rendall looked down at her with a sharp, disapproving glare, but the queen ignored him, keeping her worried gaze on Cristhian.

"She will be meeting us for dinner. We will have much to discuss." Cristhian wanted to make sure he had a moment to sit the king down and explain the entirety of the situation to him before they dealt with this…en masse.

He would make it clear to the king that Cristhian did not care what lands he ruled, these children would be Cristhian's responsibility alone.

Cristhian turned his attention to the one person who hadn't spoken yet. He smiled at Beaugonia, but she decidedly did not smile back. "Zia will be most happy to see you, Princess."

And still Zia's sister didn't speak or look upon him any less suspiciously. No doubt Zia had filled her head with tales. Well, so be it.

He didn't need anyone's approval or acceptance. There would be a wedding. Tomorrow.

He heard a strange noise behind him, looked over his shoulder and saw Zia standing there at the top of the staircase. Her stomach was hidden by the balcony. "Beau." For a moment, there was a flash of true joy on Zia's face. Cristhian felt a strange stabbing pain in the center of his chest.

Not because he wanted to be the source of such joy. How ludicrous. It was because she'd ruined his plans. Yet again.

But he didn't scowl. He didn't chastise her. Simply because it would look poorly in front of the king and queen.

Not because he was mesmerized by that joy on her face as she ran down the stairs and approached her sister. Not because the way they wrapped their arms around each other made him feel…alone. Not because it warmed him to watch them sway in each other's arms like long-lost friends. So much joy between them, Cristhian could almost feel it himself.

He smiled in spite of himself, in hope for a future where his children greeted each other in just the same way.

Certainly not any hopes for himself in there.

The king and queen clearly did not share this joy. The queen's eyes were as wide as saucers. The king looked as though he was ready to call for some beheadings.

Because Zia had ruined that gentle announcement Cristhian had planned.

Oh, well. Cristhian had to force himself to look away from Zia's happiness and turned to face the king. "You see now, sir, why I called you all here. And why a wedding will be happening tomorrow."

The joy Zia felt at seeing Beau was immediately tempered not just by her parents standing there, but also by Cristhian's heavy-handed proclamation. By the reality of this situation. Because it wasn't Beau coming to save her.

It was Cristhian following through with his…utter ridiculousness.

She didn't know why she'd allowed herself to be fooled by the past two days of quiet, of spending no time with him. She didn't know why she'd been foolish enough to think avoiding him was a punishment to him.

The way it had felt to her. Because she'd missed their conversations, his presence. And she didn't know what to do with that.

Any more than she knew what to do with her father standing there. Looking angry and threatening. Because Cristhian had *brought* him here.

So he wasn't at all concerned with if she was afraid of her father or not, even though he'd asked that question and seemed so…genuinely concerned.

What a fool she was. But she couldn't let herself wilt

under the grief of that. She had her babies to protect. From everyone.

"There will be no wedding," Zia said firmly, though maybe all that firmness was undercut by how hard she held on to Beau. "I don't know what he's told you, Father—"

"That is enough, Zia," the king said, speaking over her. "Cristhian and I will discuss this matter in private."

Zia looked at Cristhian then, wondering what the hell he thought he was doing. But his expression was carefully blank. She knew he was controlling, that he thought he knew best. She knew he could be *like* her father, but surely he wouldn't honestly secret off with her father and handle things without her having *any* say?

"Very well," Cristhian said, pointing toward the hallway. "Follow me, sir."

The king stormed after Cristhian and Zia was left with her mother and her sister, a few staff members she didn't recognize. And the sinking sensation that she was drowning. In a world she'd thought she'd escaped.

A young woman among them cleared her throat. "I'd be happy to show the queen and the princess to their suite."

"Beau will stay with me," Zia said, blinking away the tears, the utter disappointment in Cristhian.

"But Mr. Sterling said—"

"The princess will be staying in my suite with me," Zia interrupted, using all her royal training to sound as commanding as Cristhian no doubt did. She smiled at the woman though, trying to sort through all her conflicting feelings.

Because as much as her heart ached, she blamed herself for that. For having some sort of hope when it came to the man she'd somehow…trusted. But why? Why had she trusted him when he'd shown her, over and over again, exactly what he was?

But mixed in with all that disappointment was utter relief. Because Beau was here, and if Beau was here that meant Zia could find a purpose in all this pain. "The three of us will have tea in the conservatory, if someone will bring it up?"

The woman nodded and quickly disappeared.

"Follow me," Zia said to her mother and sister, heading for the stairs.

"Zia. You cannot just…take us to some conservatory and not address the…the…the issue at hand," her mother sputtered.

"Which is?" Zia asked innocently. Beau made a sound that Zia knew was her coughing to try to cover up a laugh. Because this was familiar ground. Her and Beau against the world. It would be okay. They would find a way to make it okay together.

They linked arms and Zia started up the stairs, but Beau looked back to make sure Mother was following. The queen was not happy, but she was following.

Beau leaned close. "He lives in a castle," she whispered.

"Right? He calls it a cottage. What rot."

Beau laughed again, earning them a sharp look from their mother. It was so familiar Zia almost felt herself relax. She led them both into the conservatory, offering seats. Beau took one immediately, but Mother didn't. She stood at the entrance to the room, shaking her head.

"Zia, I do not understand any of this. What has happened?"

Zia considered different versions of the truth but decided to go with the most simple and straightforward. "Cristhian and I met months ago. During—what did you call it?—my *responsibility vacation* we…hit it off. When I learned I was pregnant a few months after, I did not know how to find him. Or break it to Father. Or anyone, frankly. So I ran away."

"Pregnant," Mother echoed. "By some man you didn't even know."

Mother made it sound like she'd murdered someone in cold blood, and maybe in Mother's world it was all the same. A stain on the monarchy no matter what.

And that was all that mattered, wasn't it?

"I know him now well enough," Zia said, trying to be gentle about it. How could she blame her mother for being shocked and appalled? Cristhian had dumped this on them with no warning.

"And I suppose in some strange twist of fate, I have Father to thank for that." Was it a thank-you in her current predicament? It didn't feel it. "When Father hired Cristhian to track me down, Cristhian did not know who I was. Until he recognized me. He did not know about the babies until he found me and—"

"Babies? Zia." Mother sat then, all but collapsing into the chair, her hand to her heart. "Twins."

"Yes," Zia agreed. "Twins." She gave Beau a little smile, because especially now she was so grateful her children would have each other.

"My pregnancy was horrible," Mother said, almost

to herself. She even placed a hand over her stomach. "I was so sick. So afraid. Constantly on bed rest. It was why we never had more children though your father would have liked a boy."

Zia smiled thinly. Mother had regaled them of tales of her terrible pregnancy, but she tried not to think of that. Or the boy that they all believed would have made their lives better. "Mine has been very uneventful. The doctor tells me all the time how lucky I am that we're all so healthy."

"Yes. Incredibly so." Mother finally looked at her. *Really* looked at her. Her eyes filled. "Zia, darling, why would you keep something like this from me?"

Zia watched her mother fight back the tears, fascinated. Mother cried quite a lot, really. Always in private, of course. The *public* mask of Queen Rendall was impenetrable, emotionless. Grace and detachment above all else.

Zia never confused the two faces her mother wore, they were so intrinsically different. The public, perfect queen the king demanded. And the interior woman so afraid of going against him.

But right now, in this moment, Zia felt confused. She had expected recriminations—no doubt that would come. She had expected her mother's upset…but over the public image. Over the king's reaction.

Not Zia not *telling* her. There were so many things over the years she hadn't shared with her mother.

Namely, for one reason. "How could I tell you? I knew how Father would react. Which meant that would be how you would react as well. So I had to handle things on my own."

"Your own?" Mother scoffed, narrowed her eyes at Beau. "I hardly think so."

But before any more discussion could be had, two staff members entered with trays and quietly and quickly set up the tea for three women, then disappeared. Zia moved forward to pour, but Mother waved her off.

"Well. We must focus on the current situation we are in, not a past that cannot be changed. A small intimate ceremony is necessary for your condition, of course, but there must be *some* royal formality."

Zia watched her mother pour the tea gracefully, while Beau piled her plate high with a little bit of everything food-wise. Zia had been starving, but now her appetite left her.

"Mother. I don't care what Cristhian says, what he thinks he's planning with Father. I will not be marrying him."

"Zia." Mother set the tea pot down with a *clank*. "You're *pregnant*."

"Oh, you don't say."

But Mother was so worked up, she didn't even send Zia a censuring glance. Or Beau one when she laughed. She stood instead, wringing her hands together. "You must marry. And you'll have to stay out of sight for… Oh, I don't even know how long. No one can know…" She trailed off again, but the wringing hands certainly didn't stop. "Your father…" Again she trailed off.

"Alternatively," Zia replied, trying to maintain her calm and composure. There was really no point in lashing out at her mother. She was simply a vessel for Father's wants and desires. "I will not marry, but I can happily stay out of sight…forever."

"You're the heir," her mother said, so *scandalized* and *horrified* that being an heir might not be something Zia was going to prioritize. Not over her children.

Children. She settled her hand over her stomach. She knew her mother meant well, and yet she had caused harm to both Zia and Beau. Was that the curse of a mother? No matter how hard you tried, you would hurt your children?

Would twenty-some years down the line the two little lives growing inside her look at her and wonder why she'd denied them a legacy? Parents who were married? Or would her loving them be enough?

Because Cristhian had talked about loving his parents, and she was sure he did. Sure they sounded lovely and loving. But sometimes the image of them sounded... too good to be true. Or at least, the story as told from a child, which he had been when he'd lost them.

"I heard this crazy rumor that the king gets to choose whatever heir he likes," Beau said, interrupting Zia's thoughts on motherhood. The doubts that continued to creep up, no matter how certain she was in her choice of action.

Should she marry Cristhian...for them? Would that create a kind of insulated safety? He *was* controlling, but he claimed to want the children to come first. That was certainly not in her parents' vocabulary.

Mother whirled on Beau and shot her a sharp look. "I told your father we should leave you at home."

"What's-his-name insisted I come. He was quite adamant," Beau said, sniffing a sandwich before taking a delicate bite.

Zia stared at her sister, more than surprised by this

information. Beau didn't really need to be here, and it *was* highly unlikely either parent had wanted her here. Had Cristhian insisted...for her? "He did?"

Beau looked at her speculatively. "Yes. That's what Father said anyway. He made certain I knew I wasn't wanted on this trip."

Zia sat back in her chair and closed her eyes. Oh, what kind of idiot was she? It didn't matter. Cristhian was trying to force her into a wedding. Any gesture that seemed kind was either by accident or to purposefully get under her defenses.

She couldn't keep falling for that. "Well, we are all here now. And now we must decide how to proceed." She couldn't capitulate to Cristhian now. It would be like capitulating to Father. "Because I will not marry him. No matter what Cristhian says. No matter what *Father* says."

"You were going to marry the crown prince, Zia," Mother pointed out. "How is this different? A step down, of course, but—"

"A step down?" Zia scoffed, then inwardly berated herself for defending Cristhian when she had no reason to. But at least she had *chemistry* with Cristhian. At least they'd had conversations and...well, sex. If she was going to marry anyone...

But she wasn't. "Mother. I appreciate that me not marrying might make things...difficult for Father. But he is the *king*. I'm sure he'll weather the storm, and as Beau said, choose whatever heir he likes in the wake of me abdicating."

The queen just kept shaking her head. "You must marry the father of your children. They must be legitimate. They have kingdoms to inherit, Zia. How can you be so selfish?"

Selfish. Yes, that kept being used against her, and maybe it was fair. She did not know how to deny it. She wanted *some* things for herself. Some agency. Some freedom. Maybe that was just as wrong as her mother bowing and scraping. She genuinely didn't know.

She just knew she could not bow. She could not scrape. For herself, maybe, but first and foremost for her children.

Her children would not suffer. *They* would not be made to bow and scrape. Maybe Cristhian wouldn't expect that of them, but he was currently meeting with a man who would. Who would try everything to have an influence over them if Cristhian did not stand up to him here and now.

She had to protect them, just as she had protected Beau for all these years. It was her responsibility.

"The kingdom *I* am meant to inherit has only ever been a threat and punishment used against me." She met her mother's gaze then. "I will not do the same to my children. Maybe that is a mistake—"

"Maybe?"

"But it is my mistake to make."

Mother shook her head. "You fancy yourself very strong and very modern." Tears were in her eyes again. "You'll stand up to your father, to the world that built you?" She laughed. Bitterly. "They will crush you, Zia. I don't know why I could never teach either of you that bending keeps you from getting crushed."

"Why is bending better than crushed?" Beau asked. And Zia wanted to know the answer, but she also knew it wasn't the time to ask. One of those differences between the two of them. One of those reasons Beau would not be named heir. *Timing* wasn't in her vocabulary.

But Lille *was* modern enough. Father did have the right and law behind him to choose an heir of his own making. Maybe he wouldn't like it, but it did not *have* to be Beau replacing her.

So why did she feel so guilty? Why did bending suddenly seem like it was on the table? Because if she bent… Beau wouldn't suffer. If Cristhian could bend a little to keep her father out of this, perhaps the children wouldn't suffer.

Could she find compromise in a man who seemed to have none?

Mother shook her head, whirled around and exited the room in a huff.

Zia closed her eyes, wishing she could take a nap. Instead, she had to leverage herself up out of this chair. "I should show Mother to her room."

But Beau put a hand over her arm. "She'll find some staff person to do it. Long before we get you out of that chair."

Zia laughed in spite of herself, but Beau continued.

"Because Mother is right. You can't just stand up to them, Zia. We don't have that kind of power. They *will* crush us if we try. So we're going to have to have a plan. We're going to have to escape."

CHAPTER THIRTEEN

CRISTHIAN DIDN'T CARE for the realization that the more time he spent with King Rendall, the less he liked the man. It wasn't just that he was demanding and pompous and, well, *royal* in all those negative ways Cristhian had grown up hating.

It was the way the king spoke of the women in his family. As though they were nothing more than pawns to be moved about a board. Cristhian could picture, all too easily, his mother's family talking the same way about her when she hadn't done what she'd asked, about him when he'd been an orphaned child.

It filled him with a boiling anger he knew he needed to keep control over, but it was a struggle. Another slight he could lay at Zia's feet, once this was all over and they were married.

Settled. Once everything was settled just the way he wanted, the anger, the frustration, this damn uncertainty would go away. Everyone would be safe, and he would be able to relax.

"King Rendall," Cristhian said, after the king had gone on and on about royal weddings and whatnot. "I think you've misunderstood me. You are not in charge here."

The king narrowed his eyes at Cristhian from his seat

in an luxurious overstuffed leather chair seated in the corner of Cristhian's office. "It is not customary for *anyone* to address the king in such a manner."

"I am not a subject of your country," Cristhian replied, standing behind his desk. Then smiled and tacked on a *sir*.

The king was clearly not placated. "Do you have proof *you* are the father of these children?"

Cristhian didn't let the insult land. "I will," he responded calmly.

"I suppose your name and pedigree comes with a certain amount of…reach."

Cristhian felt he was holding his own in this ridiculous back-and-forth, but this change of topic was…confusing at best. "Reach?"

"Hisla is a small country."

Cristhian had no great love for his mother's country, but he had to admit it grated to hear the king act as though it was somehow *beneath* him. "As is Lille."

"Indeed. A partnership is what I've been after in securing my heir a husband. Both political and ensuring that the best bloodlines continue." He frowned a little and drummed heavy fingers against Cristhian's desk. "I don't know what I'll do about the crown prince. Beaugonia won't do. I don't suppose you have some princess cousins who might want to marry a crown prince?"

"I couldn't tell you. I have little to no contact with my mother's family, Your Majesty. I intend to keep it that way."

"No, that won't do. You want to marry my daughter, raise these children as you see fit, but you don't understand. It is our responsibility as leaders to consolidate and protect the kind of power that will keep our families safe and profitable until the end of times. Lille and Hisla must come to a kind of…partnership. You'll need to secure agreements with your family."

Cristhian stood there and felt something so strange and out of place he didn't recognize it at first. But eventually, understanding seeped in.

He regretted this. He'd made a mistake. To involve Zia's father, her family. He knew he wasn't wrong about getting married. But he had been wrong about trying to use her own blood as a weapon against her.

Because now, more than ever, he wanted to protect her from…*this*. Power and profits, when a child's future should be about happiness. About peace. Not just *his* children's.

But Zia's.

He had no doubt, even now, Zia and her sister were up there planning rebellions. Escapes. Just as they had planned and enacted Zia's escape to the island. In this moment of King Rendall talking about power and kingdoms, Cristhian was tempted to allow them to do just that. To get away from the man who sat before him.

But if he let Zia run away, the king would find her again. Maybe not right away. Maybe Cristhian could even thwart him, but it would mean a life of constant vigilance for Zia *and* his children. A life, essentially, on the run.

And running away never solved a thing. If anything, it always ended in destruction.

At some point, Zia was going to have to see that he was offering her protection just as much as anything else by marrying her. He was trying to do right by her, even if she didn't see it. He would protect her. He would…

A strange, clutching feeling took residence in his chest. An understanding just out of reach. And an old memory from long ago.

Your family does not have power over you unless you give it to them.

They control everything.

Not me.

Cristhian stood there while King Rendall prattled on, stuck in that memory of his parents. One from not long before they died. He'd been meant to be asleep, but he'd gone to find them for some reason he could not remember now.

They were huddled on the floor of their living room in his grandparents' house in the States, a fire crackling in the hearth. His mother had been crying. She was shaking even now, but his father held her as he always did. And said those words that echoed in his mind, as if his father was reaching out from whatever great beyond and whispering them to him now.

He'd always thought his father's words were simply love talking. Cristhian still thought that, all these years later. His father had loved his mother enough to take on some sort of unearned arrogance that he could face down an entire monarchy.

Now Cristhian was following in those same footsteps.

But it wasn't love on his part. Protecting Zia was about protecting his children. If he didn't like the thought of her under King Rendall's thumb, it was because he hated bullies. Royal bullies especially. It was because he'd watched his mother struggle and did not want that for the mother of his own children. The children would watch, they would see. So it was for them.

He had believed all of that, until this very moment.

He *didn't* love Zia. Couldn't. What was there to love? He barely knew her.

Cristhian watched King Rendall's mouth move and move and move, but he heard nothing the man was blathering on about. The word *love* clattering around inside him like some kind of internal grenade.

He thought her selfish, even if she had described a childhood where at every turn she'd made some sacrifice to protect her sister. She had run away for *herself*, not their children.

He could picture her perfectly in that cozy little cabin on an arctic island. Roughing it, essentially. It was hard to convince himself that had been selfish, exactly. There had been some sacrifice involved.

But for her own gains.

Gains she hadn't attempted until she'd fallen pregnant. Then, very resourcefully, had escaped her royal chains and somehow lived for months on that tiny, isolated island. All those small, meaningful things she'd told him about doing the week she'd been exploring freedom, just to get a taste before taking on a marriage, an inheritance she didn't want, to protect her sister.

And only the appearance of their *children* had changed the course of that. Because she had put them first.

He hadn't wanted to believe that, but he'd seen her face when she'd seen Beaugonia.

That was love. Devotion. Zia was not selfish. Perhaps, if anything, she was a little too self*less*.

He blinked at this realization, at the warmth that seemed to settle over him when she smiled at him, when she let her guard down and *trusted* him. Something he'd broken now, but he'd had there for a few days.

And he heard his father's words once more.

I saw her across the room, and she was the most beautiful thing I'd ever seen. My heart stopped.

After their deaths, Cristhian had watched many videos of his father's interviews. Before and after he'd married his mother. In those first few years after Cristhian had lost them, he'd collected any and every scrap that might keep them alive to him, that might give him hope for a life beyond his mother's family's machinations.

Sometime in his teen years, he'd cut himself off. Realizing he had to focus on his future to escape his present, rather than dwell forever in a past he couldn't get back.

But that interview played in a loop in his head now. Because from that first moment of seeing Zia walk in the door at that bar, he had felt altered. And nothing had been the same since.

My heart stopped.

Something seemed to stop inside him then. Or start. Or break apart. He moved from behind his desk. "Your Majesty," he said firmly, interrupting the king's diatribe. "This is not Lille. And Zia is not your possession. I have my own money, my own power. I do not need your permission. I do not need to follow your orders. Here, you will follow mine. There will be a wedding tomorrow. You can be there, or not. But I will not be agreeing to anything with you or Lille."

King Rendall shoved to his feet. His cheeks turning a mottled shade of red. "Then you will not inherit a dime. And neither will they. Whatever marriage you think you can enact, I will invalidate."

"I don't need your dimes, sir. Your titles. I don't need any of it." He did not say it angrily. It was a simple, easy truth. "Your reach does not extend beyond your country, and we are not *in* your country."

The king *fumed*. For a moment or two, before turning on a heel and storming out of Cristhian's office.

It wasn't over, no, but Cristhian wasn't backing down. Because love or no, nothing changed what he had to do.

Protect Zia and their children at all costs.

"We have to wait until the last possible moment," Beau was saying as they got ready for bed that night. Zia had refused to attend dinner, which was perhaps petty, but she had been exhausted and known she wouldn't be up to dealing with her father *and* Cristhian.

Because already she was having doubts of her rebellion. The more excitedly Beau spoke of escape, the more tired Zia felt. The heavier her stomach seemed. Something inside her ached, and it was hard to think past it.

What kind of life was she making for her children if they ran away? What kind of life was she making for them if she stayed? And where did either option leave Beau?

"If they have time to look for you, then they could stop us," Beau continued, crawling into the huge bed next to Zia. "So we have to create some sort of trick where they *think* they know where we are, but we're on our way. That they don't come looking until the very last minute."

"Beau. Realistically. Where are we going to go? This is not as simple as it was," she said, gesturing at the very large bump under her blanket.

"What about your island? We still have that cabin for another few months."

"Even if I didn't think Cristhian would look there first, I can't go back with this." Maybe she could get by for a week or two, but soon enough the island would insist she return to the mainland until her babies were born.

Beau had her phone in her hand. "I'll come up with something," she said, the screen illuminating her face. No doubt researching all-new lives for them.

But… Zia couldn't dream of an all-new life anymore. She had to deal with the people in this one. Not just her children, but their father. "You can't find a new life for us before tomorrow."

"Before morning," Beau replied firmly. "You're not marrying that incredibly handsome monster."

Zia laughed in spite of herself. Incredibly handsome indeed. But… "He's not a monster, Beau. And…we have to face facts. Not only will I be incredibly recognizable now that Father knows I'm pregnant, I need access to a doctor. I need lots of things, Beau. I can't fly under the radar like I did. I know I said I needed help, but…"

"Zia." Beau turned to her side to give Zia a stern look. "You can't actually be considering marrying him."

But she was. Ever since tea with Mother, she hadn't been able to completely eradicate the idea of…just letting this happen.

"Mother was right. I was ready to marry Lyon. I never expected to marry for love. I never expected to have freedom. I want it for my children, of course, but… How can *I* give it to them? Father is a worst-case scenario. Cristhian isn't as bad as that."

She believed Cristhian at least had the potential to

care about their children more than any legacy or *blood-lines*. He'd spoken of loving parents, grandparents. He expected there to be some…taking care of and putting the children first.

That was better than Father.

"He is the children's father, Beau," Zia said, and if it sounded like she was trying to convince herself, well, so be it. "That means something."

"Why?" Beau flopped onto her back. "I'd rather go through the rest of my life without dealing with *our* father."

"Cristhian isn't like him."

"He's forcing you to marry him."

"He…" Well, he *was* doing that, so how could she feel the need to defend him? After that beautiful moment of seeing their children, listening to their heartbeats, coming together again… He'd insisted on marriage. Without any care or concern about her.

He'd brought her parents here against her will. *And insisted Beau come along, too.* He'd once said he'd like to meet Beau because of the picture Zia painted.

Zia closed her eyes. She'd rather just sleep it all away. Wake up and maybe she'd have some new grand understanding of what was going on inside her.

"Zia, do you have feelings for him?" Beau asked carefully.

Zia wanted to deny it. She even opened her eyes and then her mouth, sure she could get the words out. But none came.

He was so very heavy-handed. So certain he knew what was right. Controlling.

And sometimes, she saw flashes of why. A boy who'd

lost his parents at a young age, been thrust into someone else's world. He was trying to make his own world where he could never be upended again.

And she'd upended him. The children had upended him. But he hadn't gone to sleep and hoped it would all be better in the morning. He'd made decision after decision. Wrong decisions at times, but wasn't that better than her? Letting everyone else make the decisions for her.

Even when she'd first found out she was pregnant, she'd let Beau take the reins. Beau had planned her escape, essentially, and kept her going.

Cristhian hadn't disowned his soon-to-be children. Hadn't marched her back to Lille and her father, even though that's what he'd been hired to do. No, he'd taken control of that situation by insisting they work together. Put the children first.

Was that really as bad as she was making it out to be? When he also made her heart hammer in her chest? When there was this physical chemistry that made every rational thought leave her?

Shouldn't she *want* to put the children above herself, like her mother never had? And wouldn't having two parents be better than…a mother who'd run away from their father? A mother who'd had not *one* good example of what being a good parent looked like, when their father had many?

It was enough to make her want to go to Cristhian and the minister right now and say *I do*.

But she was so worried she would become like her own mother. A shell of a person living only for the king. Or, in this case, Cristhian and *his* decisions.

And still… "I suppose I do have some sort of feelings for him," she said after a while, choosing each word carefully. "I'm not sure what they are. They're so jumbled. I'm so angry at him for pushing this marriage nonsense, and yet… I think… He speaks of his parents so… lovingly."

Zia swallowed. Beau was the only one in her whole life she could be fully honest with. Because Beau was honest back. Too blunt about it sometimes, but still. No games. No machinations. *Real*.

"It makes me think he knows what it takes to be a good parent, and that he'll be one. Maybe I need that."

"You'll be a good parent."

Beau said it with such confidence, but Zia had almost none. The closer she got to actually bringing them into the world, the more she worried how she would ever be the kind of mother that inspired the kind of feelings Cristhian had for his own. "How can you be so sure?"

"If you think he will be a good one because he had a good example, by the same logic, you will be a good one because you will know to do the opposite of our bad example."

Zia chuckled in spite of herself. It was impossible to argue with Beau's logic, but… The very simple truth was she did not know the correct course of action beyond what she did *not* want to happen.

Could she run away with Beau, somehow raise two children, free of all the controlling men in her life, and still give everyone what they deserved?

Beau needed freedom, too. She'd been dealing with their parents alone for months now. She deserved her own shot at something besides the palace and overbearing rules.

"We will be together, no matter what I decide. You aren't going back there. I promise you."

Beau was quiet for a long minute. "Zia, the truth of it all is, you care deeply about everyone and try to protect them. Maybe too much sometimes, but it is not like *our* mother. She is not evil, I know, but the only thing she has ever sought to protect is the peace. Sometimes, you need the fight. Sometimes bending *isn't* the answer, even if you get crushed."

Beau's hand found hers under the covers as she continued. "Those babies are lucky to have you as a mother, no matter what you decide. But I think you need to stop making decisions based on what's best for me."

Zia squeezed Beau's hand, turned to her in the dark. "But you can escape. Use my wedding to Cristhian as a diversion." At least that would make it worth something then. "You can take this as *your* freedom."

Beau squeezed her hand back. "You know I can't."

She didn't agree with her sister, but she understood to an extent. Beau never knew when a panic attack might hit, which made it harder to be on her own. Especially if she was trying to hide.

"At some point, you have to face yourself, Zia. Not me. Not your babies. *You.* Long after your children are born and grown, you'll still be around, and then what? Who will you be when there's no one left to protect?"

The words made Zia teary-eyed. And scared. Facing herself? When she didn't understand herself outside of those hard lines she'd grown up bowing under? When the only role that had ever made any sense to her was to protect her sister?

She swallowed at the lump in her throat. "What if I don't know how?"

Beau's hand squeezed even tighter. "I guess it's time we both figured it out."

CHAPTER FOURTEEN

CRISTHIAN DID NOT sleep well. Too many things working against him. Old memories. New problems. Threats from a king. The look on Zia's face when he'd insisted they marry.

And though that haunted him most of all, or at least tied with his father's words repeating in his head like some kind of ominous guilty conscience, he began to make the arrangements.

Maybe Zia would hate him for eternity, but he would protect her. As his father had once protected his mother. She didn't have to like it or appreciate it for the course of action to be correct.

And if he was concerned that love was clouding his judgment, he set aside for after the wedding. When everything was settled and organized, and he could work through it all and twist it to his specifications. He would not *run away* from anything. He would make sure everything… worked. Everything made sense. *Everything* protected.

He needed to find the king to lay out the consequences of his actions. To explain what would happen, and what wouldn't happen. But the queen had insisted King Rendall was not in their suite, and none of the staff had seen him, so Cristhian searched his own grounds trying not to let frustration take hold.

He was nearing the wing with Zia's set of rooms, and his mood darkened even further at the thought King Rendall was bothering her. No, this would end *now*.

But before he made it to the door to Zia's suite, the king appeared in the hallway, exiting a mostly unused library.

He stopped, gave Cristhian one disgusted look, then stormed up to him. "I will agree to the wedding. Our lawyers will call yours. Once paternity is proven, everything will be sorted from a financial standpoint." His scowl turned into something closer to a sneer. "You and Zia will be free from any responsibility to the kingdom of Lille."

Cristhian could not remember a time in his adulthood when he'd been left as utterly speechless as he was now. He hadn't even made any of the arrangements that would impress upon the king he needed to agree for Zia's sake.

What had happened?

The king stormed away before Cristhian could find his voice. Could find any sense in this strange change of heart. He snorted to himself at the idea of King Rendall having a heart.

But then he heard a strange noise. Almost like a gasp. Strangled breathing? He poked his head into the room and saw a figure huddled in a corner amid covered furniture, arms wrapped around her knees.

Zia's sister. Who was struggling to breathe, clearly. Shaking like a leaf.

No doubt over something the king had done as this

was the room he'd come out of all blusteringly angry. Cristhian strode forward.

"What did he do to you?" he demanded.

Beaugonia's body jerked in surprise, and her head came up with a snap. Her eyes were wild with something he could only call panic. But she shook her head, wiping the tears off her cheeks with the sleeve of her shirt, even as her arms shook. "N-n-nothing."

"This is not nothing."

No, it was a very large something that had more of his old memories surfacing from wherever in his psyche he'd packed them away as he'd stepped into adulthood.

All those times he'd simply thought his mother... *emotional*, he supposed, it had been more, hadn't it? More serious. More...this.

Whatever this was.

And every time his mother had behaved in this way, Cristhian had a clear memory of his father sitting next to her, taking her hand in his. He would press a kiss to her forehead, brush a hand over her hair, then tell her a story in low, calming tones. The same kind he had always delivered bedtime stories with.

As Zia's sister sat there, shaking and struggling to breathe easily, Cristhian knew he could not leave her. Even to fetch Zia or a staff member. He swallowed, then lowered himself to the ground next to her.

He wasn't sure how any of this would be received considering she no doubt viewed him as the enemy, but he took her hand anyway. It was cold, shaking. He tried to warm it in his. And when she didn't immediately pull away, or scramble away, or scream, he patted her hand.

He cast back to his memories. His father had always

spoken to his mother. Told her stories. Movie stars he'd met. A ridiculous stunt he'd done. Cristhian hadn't realized it at the time, but now he realized it was to take his mother's mind off of whatever was upsetting her.

So Cristhian figured he should do the same, even if he did not know what upset Beaugonia, or anything about her, he knew one thing. She loved her sister.

So he started there.

"I met your sister at a bar." He could see it so clearly, even all these months later. "She walked in, her hair all cut off, dyed a ridiculous attempt at red. She was even wearing colored contacts. The blue eyes didn't look right, I knew that even then. And still, even with all that fake, she swept through me like a storm." He supposed he did not need to be giving the woman *quite* so much truth.

But he thought it was helping. Maybe he was delusional. "She asked the bartender for a menu. The bartender was clearly annoyed, so I offered a suggestion. I bought her the drink. We…talked. Of work responsibilities and freedom."

He had turned that conversation over and over in his head for those months between meeting her and seeing her again. And now he understood why she had been celebrating freedom, and dreading responsibility.

Now he understood in a way he hadn't let himself up until now that this was not the action of a selfish woman. No matter how much easier it would be if he believed that of her.

"Then she invited me to go dancing with her."

"I c-can't p-picture you d-dancing."

"Ah, but I am a fantastic dancer," Cristhian returned, pretending to be offended. "Your sister certainly thought so."

Beaugonia didn't laugh, but her mouth curved a little and some of the shaking seemed to have subsided. Her breathing was coming a little easier, and no more tears tripped over onto her cheeks.

"K-keep going," she said, then she met his gaze. "I w-want to hear it all from your p-point of view."

So he sat there on the floor, and told Zia's twin the entire story—from then to now.

With Beau nowhere to be found, Zia began to worry. Because her sister was no doubt up to something. Especially considering her parents would not come out of their suite to talk to her. And now she couldn't find Cristhian.

Something was definitely happening. Not even the staff could help her track down Cristhian, which felt so ominous nausea started roiling in her stomach. She had made almost a full circle upstairs when she finally heard a low male voice.

When she came to the open door where the voice was coming from, she looked in and then froze in utter shock.

Cristhian *and* Beau. They sat next to each other. Cristhian held Beau's hand gingerly. He was speaking in calm, low tones.

Beau had clearly had a panic attack, but she was on the other side of it now. Tears had tracked her cheeks, but she was breathing normally. Maybe she was a little shaky, but not the full-blown shakes she got in the midst of it. Her eyes weren't wild or panicked.

And Cristhian sat next to her. Right at her level, *holding her hand.* Zia's heart clutched. Because it looked like he was…comforting her. She could hear him now that she stood in the entrance to the room.

"I told myself I would not track her down after she left. It had only been meant to be that one night," he was saying. Like he was telling a story.

But Zia quickly realized it was *their* story.

"Six months, and I could not stop thinking about her. I told myself all sorts of reasons for why that was."

The same as she had done. So he hadn't forgotten about her the moment she'd left as she'd believed all this time. Convinced she was just one woman in the midst of many. He'd thought of her. Couldn't stop.

It shouldn't soften her, or she didn't think it should. But he was sitting there on the ground, clearly comforting Beau with this story of *them* in the aftermath of a panic attack. He had not left her to fend for herself, had not called staff in to deal with it. He had clearly not told her to handle herself, as Father so often did.

He'd sat on the floor and held her hand. For what? There was no clear ulterior motive. Just the fact that he might be…good, underneath all that controlling.

"And what do you think the reason was?" Beau asked, but as she looked up at Cristhian, she must have caught a glimpse of Zia, because her chin jerked and her eyes widened.

So Cristhian looked over, too. He did not have the same surprise in his reaction, but he did not answer Beau's question. He got to his feet, then using the hand that had been holding Beau's, helped her up off the floor gently.

He did not seem disgusted or horrified. Zia stood there and saw with her own eyes as he gave Beau's hand a little squeeze before releasing it.

For a moment, Beau stood there looking at Cristhian with a considering expression before she carefully turned to Zia. Beau walked over to her and wrapped her arms around Zia.

"I'm going to go lie down," she whispered into Zia's ear, holding her tight.

Zia wanted to demand to know what was going on, but she knew Beau needed a good, quiet rest after an attack. "I'll come with."

"No. I'd like to be alone for a bit." Beau looked back at Cristhian, then at Zia. She continued to whisper. "Whatever you decide, I want you to know that it's okay. *I'm* okay."

"Beau…"

But Beau released her and moved into the hallway. Zia wanted nothing more than to follow, but she knew her sister well enough to know that Beau did need the alone time now.

Cristhian approached, and Zia had to turn her attention to him. She had to clear her throat to speak, because she felt very shaken, uncertain. Confused about everything she'd just seen. "I should go after her, but she wanted to be alone."

"She was…very distraught when I came upon her," Cristhian said. Clearly being very careful about words to choose. But he had an expression on his face she didn't recognize. Something very…soft.

There was no point lying, Zia supposed. "She has panic attacks. They're often brought on by…stressful social situations." But there was nothing social going on, except dealing with Cristhian, she supposed. But Beau was usually fine with anyone one-on-one. "I cannot fathom what might have brought this one on."

"Your father was in the room with her before I got here. I do not know what was discussed, but he was angry and she upset."

Zia's expression darkened. "Well, that will do it." She was glad she had a lifetime of learning how to handle her temper and she no longer went tearing into her father after one of his arguments with Beau.

That had always ended badly for Beau in the long run. He'd often made Beau even more a prisoner in the castle after that. Kept Zia from seeing her. Kept anyone from seeing her until Beau could "handle herself."

So Zia had learned to keep her anger internalized. Plan little rebellions. Ones that had no chance of hurting Beau.

And for the past few months, while Beau had been helping her with her own, who had Beau had? No one. Zia couldn't take back protecting her children, but what she *could* do was make decisions in the here and now that did both things.

Zia would get Beau out of this. She looked up at Cristhian…who had been kind in the face of Beau's panic attack. She could tell from the position she'd found them in, from Beau's reaction.

But he was looking at the door, a strange frown on his face. "Panic attacks."

Zia braced herself for an insensitive comment. The ones her parents and their staff had leveled at Beau her whole life. Cristhian had been kind to Beau's face, but there was no way he could understand—

"It was so familiar," he said, as if in a kind of trance. "I think… My mother had them. I simply thought she was crying, but it was like that. The shaking, the struggling to breathe. I never understood. I don't know if *they* did." He said it like he was lost in some old memory.

And was potentially realizing his mother might have been a real and complex person, even if his memories were from a child's perspective of simplifying things. But children knew. They understood the world around them, often better than adults understood, or at least differently.

Cristhian was clearly having a moment of clarity, and she yearned to give him more, if she could. "Do you think they were brought on by her leaving her family?" She certainly wouldn't be having any panic attacks about that, but maybe it was more complicated than she was giving it credit for.

"She never fully left. They wouldn't allow it. Even disapproving of my father, they did not want to lose their control over her completely. So she struggled with the way they treated her. So often they tried to stir up false stories. Infidelities. Abuse. My parents never believed these things, and the media never could seem to make the accusations stick, either. It was all…mind games, but the complications went away if she attended the events they wanted. I always thought her reaction was just the stress. I have always blamed her family for pushing at her, tearing at her, but some small part of me… I have always felt guilty of it, but deep down I blamed her, too. For running instead of standing up to them."

Zia watched him, surprised to find this moment of

pure vulnerability. He was coming to some new conclusions and allowing her to be a part of it. She wanted to reach out and comfort him, and she would have held herself back. Even now, she would have held herself back.

But he'd comforted Beau. So she reached out and took his had in hers, as he had done for her sister.

"Sometimes running away is the only option we have. Sometimes, there is no standing up, no matter how much we'd like to."

He looked at her then. Still caught up in his past, but she knew he saw the connection, and because she did, she felt even softer toward him. She had never realized until this moment, and maybe he had not fully either, just how much *running* represented something horrible to him.

"I did not realize that perhaps she was not able to stand up to them," he said, his voice low, strained. "No matter how she tried. And my father tried. To protect her from it, but he couldn't, either. Because it wasn't them. It was her."

She tried to drop his hand. Every time she thought she glimpsed some human part of him… "People are not to blame for the ways their brains and bodies betray them."

But he squeezed her hand so she could not pull away. And then he held it gently. So gently it seemed wrong to pull her arm away.

"No, that is not how I mean it, Zia. I did… I think. I loved my mother more than anything, but still I blamed her for that. Somewhere. Deep down. Until I saw your sister and understood." He swallowed, as if some deep emotion was clogged there in his throat.

Which in turn made her own throat feel tight. That a man so bent on control could acknowledge that maybe…

maybe he was not always right, maybe he didn't *always* understand every little thing.

"No one could protect my mother, and that was wrong. My father tried with all he was, but he couldn't… He wasn't given the time to accomplish this goal," he said, some conviction and strength returning to his voice. "I know you don't want to marry me. I understand you think I will rule your life as your father has. But, Zia, I will protect you. I will protect our children. I will protect Beaugonia and anyone else you'd like me to."

Her heart began to beat double time in her chest. She knew he could lie if he wanted to, but he spoke with a fervency she did not know how to take as anything but truth. The kind of promise she'd never been given before.

"I can make certain we marry, Zia. I can make certain I protect you no matter what. But if you could see my side of things, it will be easier. For everyone. If you can agree, without a fight, without an escape attempt, we can make a world that is better for our children than what we ended up with."

She should be offended that he thought she couldn't say no, that she couldn't escape, no matter what, but he was talking to something bigger now. Protection.

Of the babies. Of Beau. Of *her*.

These were words and promises she'd wanted. These were words that made everything she needed to do okay. Her babies and Beau free of her father. It should be enough, but…

"Because you hate what royalty did to your mother? Because you could not protect her, and she could not protect you?"

His dark eyes studied her, like he was taking in every

line and curve of her face. So much so she thought maybe
there would be…some other answer. Maybe she even
held her breath hoping for some *more*.

"Yes."

It was less than she wanted from Cristhian, and still
more than she'd dared hope for when it came to a future
marriage. It was what she'd tried to live her life for. To
protect Beau, and then these babies once she'd learned
of them. So how could she say no? He was offering her
a way out of the walls that had held her and the people
she loved captive.

Maybe there would be new walls involved, but in protecting everything she held dear, did it matter? He was
offering more than she'd had under her father's thumb,
and maybe in that there would be some space for her
own say.

"All right." She tried to manage a smile, but couldn't
quite get there. "I'll marry you."

CHAPTER FIFTEEN

CRISTHIAN HAD ALREADY made certain all the wedding plans were in place. He had foreseen no circumstance where the wedding would *not* happen. But now that Zia had agreed, he expected to feel an even stronger sense of certainty. He would not have to thwart any escapes or overcome any overzealous nos.

Everything should be fine and settled with her agreement and everyone in the household on the same page.

If anything, as he got word the minister would be arriving shortly, he felt the opposite. As though her saying she would marry him without incident harvested an entire field of doubts inside him.

Which was ridiculous. Marriage was the right course of action. And he would protect her, their children, her sister. Anyone else. From all that the monarchy so carelessly hurt.

That was the legacy his father had left him.

And look how that turned out.

He shook his head. They weren't running away. If anything, they were standing up to the pressures. Just as he had done as a young man, extricating himself from a family who had never cared about anything other than their own reputations.

He was taking that need to run away from her. *For* her. In all the ways he'd been too young to do it for his parents.

He had been a success ever since he'd stepped away from his mother's family. So how could getting Zia away from hers not be a success?

And the king had agreed. Even now, their lawyers were hashing out the details. All necessary agreements would be completed and signed before the small ceremony tonight.

But what had caused the king's change of heart? Something to do with Beaugonia. It had to be. The timing made no sense otherwise. Which was really none of his business.

So he tried to convince himself. Still, the worry, the confusion, the frustration lingered.

If whatever had gone on between the king and Beaugonia hurt Zia…

Eventually, Cristhian could not stand it any longer. He had one of his staff members hunt down Beau and bring her to him. Without Zia.

It took longer than he would have liked. First his lawyers swept in with their concerns and paperwork. Things the king had tried to sneak by them, things they had tried to sneak by the king. But in the end, Cristhian had what he wanted.

A legal guarantee Zia would not be required to fulfill any royal duties she did not wish, that their children would make their own decisions on if they would like titles or not. A small and, to Cristhian's mind, unnecessary inheritance, but he wouldn't fault the king for that.

All would go into place once he and Zia were married,

and then all would be just as Cristhian wanted it. Everyone protected as he saw fit. By the law and his own hand.

And still no sense of calm came over him.

When Beaugonia was ushered into his office, he was certain once he dealt with her, he would feel it. She was the last loose thread.

"Good afternoon, Cristhian," she offered cheerfully, though he didn't fully believe the cheer. "It seems you are in desperate need of my company."

"I have an important question to ask you, Your Highness." He walked over to the door, closed and locked it himself. Beaugonia looked at the knob with great suspicion, so Cristhian stayed by the door rather than approach her. It was not his goal to make her uncomfortable.

But he had to know the truth.

"I would like to know what you and your father discussed this morning that had such an…effect on you."

Beau looked him up and down, head cocked to one side. "Too bad."

For a moment, he couldn't speak. When he did, he was alarmed to find his voice had raised an octave. "I beg your pardon."

"I don't want you to know. So you won't. Not yet, anyway." Then she shrugged. As if that was that.

He supposed he finally saw some of the resemblance between the two sisters. Stubbornness in direct opposition to his goals.

"Princess—"

"You saw me through a panic attack, Cristhian. I think you can call me by my name."

It was hard to reconcile this self-possessed woman with the woman from this morning, shaking and struggling to breathe, the one he'd initially met who hid behind her parents and didn't speak. And yet he'd always seen his mother as a whole, complicated woman, hadn't he? Sometimes she was upset, and sometimes she had it all handled. She was not all one thing.

Perhaps none of them were all *one* thing.

"Beaugonia," he said then, keeping his gaze on hers. A firmness in his tone so she could understand he was serious and would not be deterred. He needed answers. With answers, everything would be sorted. "Your father had a seemingly miraculous change of heart after charging out of that room. I would like to know what caused it, and if it might affect Zia in some way that she is not aware of."

Beau didn't react to this right away. She stood, still and blank-expressioned. Then she turned away from him, walking around his office, poking at books on shelves, papers on his desk. She settled herself at the window, looking out over a world of white.

"Everything I do is for my sister," she said at last. "For the entirety of my life, she has put herself in front of me like a human shield. Because I was different and couldn't be what our parents wanted me to be. Well, I'm old enough, clever enough and aware enough now to deal with all that. Strong enough to be the one shielding Zia this time around, so she can protect those children." She met his gaze then, direct and determined. "I would do anything to keep my parents from having any influence on another generation."

"I may not know your sister as well as you do, but I can assure you, she wouldn't want you to sacrifice yourself for anything."

"No," Beaugonia said with a smile. But it didn't last long. Her mouth curved back into a frown. "But I didn't always want her to protect me at great cost to herself. Helping someone isn't always about *wants*. I suppose that's love, all in all."

Love. Cristhian did not like how this topic kept coming up, how it seemed to root him to the spot. Like an anchor.

Drowning him? It should feel like it was drowning him, against his will. But he had a strange new thought then. An anchor didn't drown. It tethered. Kept a boat secured to an important shore.

And if love…could be an anchor. If he loved Zia, told her that, would she stay tethered to his very important shore?

What the hell was wrong with him thinking in boat analogies?

But then Beaugonia crossed the room to him. She stopped a few feet away, but he could see Zia stamped all over her. The soft cast of her mouth, the intelligence behind her eyes. All behind a very thin mask of wariness.

But willing to brave the wariness to do what needed to be done, say what needed to be said. Protect who needed protecting.

How could he not respect that?

"I think you might be a good man, Cristhian Sterling. And if you're not, I'll make sure to make you suffer. But for now, I'm entrusting you to protect Zia. And that niece and nephew of mine."

"There is nothing I take more seriously. I could protect you, too. Now, or in the future should you need it."

She smiled. "That is very kind. Zia never mentioned you were such a softy."

He scowled a little at that, and she laughed, reminding him of Zia.

"Should I need it, I'll take you up on that help. But for now, I need you to leave this. To make Zia leave it as well. These are the things I need to do for my sister, with no interference. Please."

Cristhian normally would have left nothing. Not for anyone.

But with *love* rattling around inside him, some unwieldy thing, he could only nod and let Beaugonia go.

Zia had needed a nap before she was to start getting ready for the wedding. She hadn't slept well last night due to stress, and the aches and pains of pregnancy were really announcing themselves because of it.

It was just the stress of everything. The doubts. The fear she was making a mistake. The fear she was doing what was right, what needed to be done, and it would still somehow turn out all wrong.

The loop of wondering if thinking you knew what the right thing to do was an endless generational curse on your children.

And worse, so much worse, silly little fantasies about somehow...somehow creating a real marriage with Cristhian. Something with chemistry and trust and partnership and...love.

Oh, honestly. Could she be more foolish?

She maneuvered her way up and out of bed. She had to pause once she was standing, breathe deeply a few times through all the anxiety making breathing feel harder than it should. That and two babies squishing up against her lungs making it impossible to take a full breath. Every day it seemed a little bit more impossible that this could go on for *weeks*.

And still she wasn't eager for the alternative. She took a step, a sharp pain lodging itself in her side. Sort of like a cramp after running too hard and long. And certainly too far to the side to be anything involving the children. She'd probably pulled a muscle or something while she was sleeping, or maybe when she'd struggled to get up off the bed.

She took another step and the pain loosened a little, so she went in search of Beau. But as she went from room to room in their suites, she was nowhere to be found. She couldn't find her mother, either, which was odd since they had said they would be ready to help her get ready once she woke up.

She searched the entire upstairs to no avail. The pain in her side pretty much disappeared, until she started going down the stairs. Then it started up again. She stretched her arm up above her head, moved around a bit, and it went away.

Once downstairs, she decided to find Cristhian, see if he knew what was going on. Staff members were scarce. Alejandra had said most of them were in the main ballroom getting it ready for the ceremony. So she went to the rooms Cristhian favored, starting with his office.

He sat behind his desk, frowning over a stack of papers. Zia stood in the entrance, simply watching him for a silent moment.

In a few short hours, she would agree to marry this man. She would commit herself to a life of…controlling behavior. He would do everything *he* thought was right, and she would have no say.

But did it matter if he was doing it to love and protect their children? He had been kind to Beau, when so many people had not been—including their own parents. Should their children struggle with something, he would be kind to them, too.

What more could she really ask for? Love? When the only love she had ever witnessed was the kind that sacrificed self over all else?

She shook her head. She had to find Beau. She had to go through with this, so Beau could escape. She would find a way to make sure Beau got out. With Cristhian's help, she could do it.

He glanced up, as if he'd sensed her there. He got to his feet, something like concern flitting over his face. "Is everything all right?" he asked when she didn't speak.

She moved a little farther into the office, trying to focus on the task at hand. "Have you seen my sister?"

Cristhian looked at her and frowned. "Are you quite all right? You're looking pale."

"Fine. Just tired. But I can't find my mother or Beau. I asked Alejandra to search for them, but it's been quite a while now and she hasn't returned either." The pain seized her side again, and she rubbed at it, taking a few more steps into his office in hopes of soothing it out.

"You couldn't find any of them?"

Zia shook her head. "Mother and Beau are supposed to help me get ready for the ceremony. I don't know where they could be."

Cristhian skirted his desk, but before he moved fully to her or said anything else, one of his staff members entered the room. The man cleared his throat.

"Sir, I am to inform you that the king and queen and the princess have left."

"Left?" Cristhian and Zia echoed at the same time.

"Yes, sir. Just now. I was just told of this and came to relay it immediately."

"Why was I not informed of their plan?" Cristhian demanded, and he seemed *very* convincing in his surprise, so Zia didn't think he was acting.

"I'm very sorry, sir. Apparently they made all of the arrangements themselves. The princess even carried their bags out to the waiting vehicle. No one knew about it until just now, when they were seen driving away."

Zia was utterly speechless, but the man turned to her. Held out an envelope.

"This was left in their rooms with your name on it, ma'am."

Zia took the envelope with nerveless fingers. It was her sister's handwriting on the outside, and on the inside as well.

Zia,

I've got this under control.

Love,

B

It made no sense. Why would Beau go off with Mother and Father? Why would any of this be happening before the wedding that was supposed to make everything all right?

"Cristhian, we have to… We have to go after her." The pain in her side was getting worse, but she tried to ignore it. "I don't know what's going on, but I prom…" She couldn't finish the word. A wave of pain seemed to clamp down on her.

Cristhian was at her side immediately. "Are you in pain? What is it?"

"Just…" But she couldn't quite get the words out. She had to grit her teeth against the wave of tension that seized her body.

"Go get the doctor," he said in harsh tones, and the man quickly disappeared.

"Cristhian." Zia was panting now, though she couldn't understand why. Maybe *she* was having a panic attack. "She can't just leave."

"Once we have you settled, I will see what I can do. But for now, we must have you checked out. Yes?" But he wasn't allowing her a chance to respond, he was just ushering her to a different room. One with a couch.

He eased her onto it. That did help, lying down. Cristhian crouched next to her, brushed some hair off her face in a move so gentle her heart stuttered.

"I promise, I will do what I can, but I think your sister had some plans of her own. I know I can't tell you not to worry about her, but I think she has a better control of whatever situation she's in than you think."

"Her letter. She said she has it under control."

Cristhian nodded, his gaze never leaving hers, his fingers still on her face.

"I believe her. Your parents have their deep, deep faults, Princesa, but they have raised two very capable women."

Zia didn't know why that made her want to cry, but the tears filled her eyes. She didn't let them fall, mostly because the doctor strode in, bag in hand. She went straight for the couch, immediately shooing Cristhian out of the way.

"What has happened, Your Highness?"

Cristhian opened his mouth, but the doctor held up a hand. "In the patient's own words, thank you."

Cristhian clamped his mouth shut, though he looked stormy and angry about it, which almost amused Zia enough to smile.

"My side was hurting," Zia told the doctor. "I thought I'd simply slept on it wrong, but it got worse."

The doctor had her point to where it hurt, asked her more questions about the pain, then enlisted Cristhian to help arrange things so the doctor could do a more in-depth exam.

The doctor made considering noises as she took different vital signs, both from Zia and from the babies, then poked around at this and that. When she was done, and she let Cristhian help Zia into a more comfortable position on the couch, she smiled at both of them.

"Everything is just fine."

The doctor's words sent a wave of relief through her, even though she still worried about Beau. About what her father thought he was doing making them all leave before the wedding even happened.

"I think I was just panicking," Zia said on a whisper.

The doctor shook her head. "Princess, you've begun to dilate, and you're having some very minor contractions. Perhaps panic played a role, but that's not the whole story. You'll want to stay in bed for the next few days. We'll monitor, make sure everything calms down. It should, but stress is to be avoided."

The doctor glanced at Cristhian, then returned her gaze to Zia and smiled. "Rest. Relax. That's the best thing for you right now. Should you have more pain, call me immediately."

Zia managed to nod at the doctor. Everything was fine. *Fine.* She placed her hands over her stomach, felt a tiny little roll against her palm. They were good.

But what about Beau?

"Once the pain is completely gone, move her up to her room," the doctor was telling Cristhian. "She should stay there. All meals brought to her. Supervision when she needs to get up. This is very common, particularly with multiples, but it'll require some more care taken from the day-to-day to make sure she isn't overtaxing herself."

"I will make certain she doesn't."

The doctor nodded. "Either of you, fetch me if you need anything." And then she was gone as quickly as she'd come.

Cristhian stood at the threshold to the room. He didn't say anything, and a long silence stretched out between them. Until Zia couldn't take it any longer.

"I suppose we'll have to postpone the wedding then."

He gave a short little nod. "Of course."

"I didn't mean for…"

"Zia." He sounded pained. "Of course you didn't. Our number one priority is that you and the children are healthy. Weddings can wait."

"But—"

"You need not worry. Doctor's orders. Trust me. I promised you. I will protect you all. Beau included."

She studied him then, and there was something different about him. A softness she had not fully seen in him before—at least before he hid it behind that arrogance and control. She understood that Beau's panic attack had made him realize things about his mother, and she supposed that's why he was offering to be so supportive of her, but...

"Why, Cristhian? I understand the children are yours, but Beau and I are not. You don't owe us your protection."

"I have never been a fan of the word *owe*. It was used against me for many years. What I *owed* my mother's legacy." He shook his head. "But what I discovered in those difficult years is that anyone's life is a tapestry. What might life have been like if my mother's family had included my father's, instead of trying to fight a war? My children will have all the pieces they can of people who will put them first. That includes their mother, and their aunt."

"Aunt," Zia repeated. She'd spent so much of the past few months trying to set up a life for her children, but she admittedly had spent little time thinking of them as...little people in the world, in *her* world. Calling Beau *Aunt*. And Cristhian *Father*.

"Family protects, or it should. So that is what we will do." He took her hand then, clasped it between his two much larger ones. "But I'm discovering there is more, Zia. Quite unexpectedly, I find myself...being in love with you."

Love. For a moment, she didn't breathe, but even when she reminded herself to, she didn't say anything.

Ever since he'd introduced the idea, what felt like forever ago but was only perhaps a week now, she had been convinced that she would allow him to fall in love with *her*. That this would be best, really. And she would stay perfectly...detached. She would use his love as a kind of safeguard, but she would not allow herself to feel that much, that deeply, so that it ended up affecting her choices when it came to their children.

So she didn't speak. Even with her heart racing in her chest, even with this strange…elation soaring through her. She didn't respond to him.

He could love her, and that would be okay. Best even.

But she would not allow herself to love him.

Ever.

CHAPTER SIXTEEN

AFTER A TIME, Cristhian helped Zia back upstairs to her room. He tucked her into bed, then began to give instructions to staff about how to proceed while she was on bed rest. Including moving some of his things into her suite.

He would be here through the night, and as long as he needed until he felt assured that all would be well. He trusted the doctor, but his brain had not yet taken the doctor's assurances on board.

Perhaps his brain was no longer functioning, since he had told Zia that he was in love with her.

She had very purposely not said it back.

This was fine, perhaps even best. It allowed him to make the right choices. Love did not need to be reciprocal to put things in their place.

He would love her, and their children, and *that* would be the settled, controlled feeling he was searching for.

So he made sure an array of foods were brought up for her to eat, a drink within arm's reach at all times, and he ignored her protests when he settled himself into a chair and insisted he would not leave until she fell asleep.

Once she finally did, he watched her for a time. The slow, steady rise and fall of her breathing. Everything was under control, because he had put everything in perfect place. The doctor on property, quick to drop in and make certain everything was okay.

Perhaps the wedding had not gone according to plan, perhaps nothing with Zia's family had, but he had rolled with every punch.

Perhaps he had not fully thought through love declarations, but what did a few words matter?

His phone began to buzz for what felt like the hundredth time. He finally pulled it out of his pocket and looked at the screen. He had quite a few messages, but he ignored all of them except the one from his grandparents. He moved out of Zia's bedroom and into one of the exterior rooms where he could make a call to them without waking Zia. They had been expecting to video into his wedding, so no doubt they were concerned they'd missed something.

His grandmother's kitchen table appeared on the screen, and Cristhian smiled in spite of himself. "Hello, Grandmother. Your camera is backward."

She muttered something, then got it to turn around so that both his grandparents' faces were on the screen.

"I apologize," he said, surprised at how stiff he sounded. "The ceremony had to be postponed. Zia begun to have some contractions. She is to be on bed rest for the next few days, and then we will reevaluate."

"How frightening for her," Grandmother said, a worried frown crossing her features.

"Indeed."

"And you."

Indeed.

She had been looking pale, pained. So worried about Beaugonia when she should be worrying about herself.

"What can we do, Cristhian?" his grandfather asked gently.

What can we do?

They had always asked that. Even when there was an ocean of impossibility between them, they had always asked what they could do. Not what *he* could do. Not what *he* could offer.

"Nothing." He smiled thinly. "But thank you. The doctor assures us all is well, and that is the most important thing now. The wedding will commence once she's better, and I'll make certain you're able to watch."

"Yes, of course. We'll watch whenever it is. But, dear, are you sure *you're* all right?"

"It has been…a stressful day."

"Tell us," Grandfather urged gently.

For much of his early adulthood, he had sat down and done just that. Dumped everything on his grandparents, and then listened to their advice. Sometimes he'd taken it. Sometimes he hadn't. But either way, he'd never been worried about their censure, and they'd always been there, ready to listen to his next conundrum, no matter the outcome of the last.

For the past few years, he had not leaned on them as much. He was an adult. In charge of his life. He worried about their health, the effect stress or worry would have on them.

But tonight, when they encouraged him to tell, he sat down and did just that. King Rendall. Beaugonia's panic attack and the clarity it gave him. Down to telling Zia he loved her. And her saying nothing back.

"Well, that is *certainly* a stressful day," Grandfather said after a bit.

"It is under control, though," Cristhian said. "Zia has agreed to marry me. Her father has agreed to let her go. All will be well."

His grandparents shared one of their looks.

"You do understand you can't control *life*, Cristhian."

Cristhian didn't have a quick return for that. It wasn't that he thought he was controlling *life*, just that if he organized things a certain way, all would be well. If he got everyone to agree to his way of things, then things would turn out the way they should.

That wasn't *control*. It was just…being in charge, being successful, not letting life knock you out. Because you were protected.

"Once we are married, everything will fall into place. Zia does care for me," Cristhian said, sure he was comforting them…and not himself. Because there was *something* between Zia and him, or they wouldn't be in this predicament.

"Cristhian, you can't *make* anyone love you. You can't perfect all the conditions so they decide to. You can only honor your own feelings and your own needs. While respecting theirs."

Cristhian tried to reject those words, but he'd never been any good at ignoring his grandparents' wisdom. They'd been there, every step they could be. The only solid points in his life along with his parents' memory.

And even that had been rocked by his realizations this morning about panic attacks. About how deep everything with his mother had gone. And now, in this moment, that someday he would not have his grandparents' wisdom to rely on.

Life and time would march on. Both too short, and infinite, all at the same time. Everything he'd been trying to control, since that moment he'd lost his parents, was an exercise in futility.

"You know," Grandmother said after the silence had stretched on too long. "I said I love you to your grandfather first and he didn't say anything back."

"That is not true!"

"It is absolutely true," Grandmother shot back. "You were so busy playing with that damn dog of yours—"

"Which means I didn't *hear* you, not that I didn't *say it back*."

"I think you heard me."

They bickered like that for a few minutes, shoulder to shoulder, smiling even as they disagreed. About events long gone. And through that time and this time, they had loved each other. Weathered storms and tragedies and challenges, alongside joys.

Cristhian had spent his life with these examples of love. So much so he'd been sure love was the answer.

And he supposed it was. But not just the words. Something bigger. Something deeper. Not love as an agent of *control*, but something far more terrifying.

"Thank you."

"For what?" Grandfather asked, confusion drawing his bushy white brows together.

"For being yourselves. It has been an invaluable part of my life." One that Zia did not have. So, no, he could not control things to ensure her feelings. But what he

could do, but what he would do, was give her something
she'd never had.

And spread that love and support to their children, no
matter where life took them.

They said their I-love-yous and their goodbyes. For a
moment Cristhian sat in the darkened room and just listened to his own breathing.

You can't make anyone love you.

Had he thought he could? No, it was more complicated than that. Perhaps he'd rested too much on the idea
that love would be the answer. That if she loved him, he
would get what he wanted.

Also simplistic, when his feelings were anything but.

He returned to her bedroom. She was still asleep.

He had received confirmation that the royal family had returned to their castle in Lille. He still did not
know what had happened, but he had decided to trust
that Beaugonia had it all under control, as she'd claimed.

And for the first time in his life since he'd lost his
parents, he had to trust that control was *not* the answer.

Letting go was.

Zia woke up. Her room was dim, the curtains drawn, but
she noted there was sunlight creeping around the edges.
She glanced at the clock. It was well into the morning.
She'd slept a ridiculous amount.

She stretched in the bed, took stock of her body. She
did feel better than she had at any point yesterday. More
herself, or at least her healthy pregnant self. She yawned
and pushed herself into a tentative sitting position, ready
for any little twinge that she thought meant she should
lie back down.

But none came. She let out a long breath of relief, then studied the dim room around her. She startled a bit when she realized there was a body on the little lounge in the corner. Cristhian. Fast asleep.

So handsome it nearly took her breath away. Had he really said he loved her, or was that some dream she'd had? Or maybe another machination. Could she put that past him?

She watched him sleep, her heart twisting in a million little knots. He had said he *loved* her, and she did not know how to take it for a lie. But *why*? She had finally agreed to marry him; he didn't need to make up stories now.

So why had he said it?

His phone vibrated in his pocket, and this seemed to wake him. He didn't notice her sitting and looking at him as he pulled his phone out of his pocket. He frowned at the screen, poked at it a few times, then shook his head.

When he looked up, he didn't register any surprise that she was sitting there watching him, but something did cross his expression. A kind of resignation. He got to his feet, walked over to the bed.

"Good morning. Did you sleep?"

She nodded.

"Zia…" He sighed, like he was about to deliver bad news. "I want to make something clear before I tell you what's happened."

"What's happened?"

But he ignored her. "We do not need to marry, if you'd rather not. We can live here, or at one of my other estates, and raise the children together. As…friends, I suppose you'd call it. We can find a way. It was wrong of me to think only marriage could accomplish this."

Her mouth dropped open, like all her facial muscles had deserted her in shock. He was admitting he was wrong? Just as she'd finally agreed to marry him, he was saying they didn't have to? *After* he'd said he *loved* her? "Why are you saying this?"

"To be clear, I think marrying would be best. I think you could learn to love me. I think we could build a family, putting our children first. Protecting them. But your sister said something to me that has stuck with me. She did not always appreciate your protection, and yet what she's done was out of love and a gratefulness for that protection. So that you would take a turn at…living your own life, I suppose. So I want you to have a chance at that life that *you* choose. Because I, too, love you."

There was that word again, and she just…didn't know what to do with it. So she focused on her sister. "What has she done?"

He handed her his phone and Zia looked at the article on the screen. The headline was in big block letters: Princess Beaugonia Rendall, Newly Minted Heir of Lille, Weds Crown Prince Lyon Traverso of Divio in Private Ceremony!

Zia could only stare, reading the headline over and over again until she finally found her voice. "She can't do that."

"It seems she already has," Cristhian said gently, taking the phone from her hand.

"But how? I don't…" Zia shook her head.

"She set you free."

So why did it feel like she was drowning? Facing

down some unknown future instead of one that was clear. "I didn't ask to be set free! I am not *free*!" Zia pushed out of bed, not sure where she thought she was going. "She is my sister. I love her, and I'm worried for her."

Cristhian stood in her way, then gently nudged her back onto the bed. Because she was on *bed rest*.

"Sit. Rest."

She did as she was told because those were the doctor's orders and she would follow them. But…how could she just lie here while her sister… She shook her head. This couldn't be true.

"Cristhian. This is why my father agreed to let me go. She took my place." She looked up at him, on the verge of tears. And his expression was sympathetic. But he simply nodded.

"Yes, that is what it looks like."

"What am I to do if…?"

At some point, you have to face yourself, Zia. Not me. Not your babies. You.

Beau had said that to her. And now she was forcing Zia to do it. Not just her, but Cristhian, too. It wasn't fair. "Why are you doing this to me?"

He cocked his head, as if he didn't understand the accusation. Maybe *she* didn't understand it either, but it felt better to demand it of him than figure out what was going on inside her.

"I don't think I am doing anything *to* you, Zia. I am giving you a choice."

She stared at him, bowled over by such a sentence. By the realization that swelled through her. "I have never had a choice. Not about anything." It was an exaggeration, she supposed. She had *chosen* to protect Beau. She had *chosen* to have her little week rebellion, then run away for good when she discovered the consequences.

But no one had ever looked at her and told her she did not have to think about consequences. She could just *choose*. And everything would be taken care of regardless of her choice.

"Not long ago, I would have scoffed at that, but I think you're right in a way. I think everything you have done has been in reaction to something. To protect someone. So here we are. With no one left to protect. Because your sister has made her choice, and I have ensured our children's protection. So it might be difficult and uncomfortable, but it is time, Zia. Make a choice for yourself."

She stared at him, completely and utterly lost. Make a choice for *her*? Without thought to anyone else? She didn't… She couldn't…

"You have time, *Princesa*. There is no rush. I thought I knew how it should all go to make it exactly right. I suppose, in a way, I've been searching for exactly right since I lost my parents. I have tried to control you, because I thought it was best. *Right.* But there is no exactly right. None to be had. So we will take whatever time we need to make every next step. Perhaps not all the right ones, but if we put our children first, they will be right enough."

He took her hand, kept saying these words that seemed to tear down all the protections she'd so carefully hung up over the years. They'd started crumbling when Beau had told her to make choices for herself, and now there was nothing left.

He'd taken it all away.

"I have not been the same since you walked into my

life, Zia. I thought I could put that into a neat little order, control it all, make it be what I wanted. That is how I am used to dealing with my life being upended."

"*My* life was upended."

"Yes. We both have been forced to face the consequences of our actions. I'm not sure either of us handled it as well as perhaps we should have, but we have not done irreparable damage. We have done our best, and now we'll do better."

"By *not* marrying?"

"By choosing, Zia. On my end, I choose you. I have fallen in love with you. Your strength and protective spirit. Your beauty and your wit. But regardless of my feelings, I think we can raise these children mostly on the same page. And that is what I vow to do, regardless of what you choose for yourself."

"Cristhian…"

"So you take your time. You think on what *you* vow to do. For yourself."

At some point, you have to face yourself, Zia. Not me. Not your babies. You.

Cristhian watched over her for the next few days, barely leaving her side, but he did not push the matter. The doctor gave her the all clear to leave bed rest, but she was cautioned to listen to her body, to watch for signs she needed to rest.

He gave her space then. They ate dinner together, but unless she requested his presence, he stayed away.

And she found it didn't take long at all to miss him. At first, she convinced herself it was just the company she missed. She was lonely.

But Beau called her every day. She wouldn't give too

much away about her new life as a married woman, but she didn't seem upset or unhappy. She seemed very much herself.

And still, Zia longed for Cristhian. There was something comforting about his presence. In so many different ways.

"So," Beau drew out, making Zia realize she'd zoned out of their conversation. "I take it you haven't decided what to do about Cristhian."

"I am still living here, aren't I?"

"That's not a decision, Zia. That's staying still hoping someone swoops in and makes the decision for you."

She wasn't hoping for that. She didn't think. "How am I supposed to just *decide* if I love him, or if I could? They are feelings. Not decisions. Not math facts."

"I am learning all sorts of fascinating things about being married to a man I barely know. One of them is this. I do not question whether or not I love Lyon. I *know* I do not."

"It isn't that simple," Zia insisted. How could it be? She had a relationship with Cristhian. It wasn't just taking on an arranged marriage.

"Hmm," Beau replied.

"It *isn't*. I'm confused because… He says he loves me, Beau, but how could he? Why would he? We only barely know each other. I have nothing to offer him, really. I can't do any protecting, play some role in his life. I am simply the mother of his children."

"Nothing to offer… Zia, it's not a *transaction*."

"No, but…"

"Zia, you don't have to be useful to him for him to love you. You know that, don't you?"

"I don't think…" But she supposed, in a way, she didn't understand why he would claim love when there was nothing she was really giving him, beyond birthing their children.

"It doesn't take Psychology 101 to determine that's a warped thought no doubt brought on by how our parents treated you as heir. I love you regardless of what you've done for me."

"You're my sister."

"Yes, and I happen to think you're smart and funny and delightfully spiteful, when you want to be. I know you'll be as wonderful a mother as you were a sister. So, again, why wouldn't Cristhian love that? You're beautiful, and clearly your chemistry is through the roof. I think these are the things normal people use to determine love."

Zia didn't have the words to answer that. Mostly because she didn't think Beau was *wrong*, per se, just… how could that apply to her? She didn't want to delve into that. "How is Lyon treating you?"

She could practically hear Beau roll her eyes at the topic change.

"Quite well, all in all. You know, I'm glad it's me, Zia. I should like to think that you would be so kind as to use the freedom I helped you accomplish to be happy."

That little remark landed a bit like a slap. "Beau."

"I have to go. Dinner waits for no crown princess and future popper-outer of heirs. I love you, Zia. For who you are. Not what you can do."

"Beau."

But the line went dead, and Zia was forced to face too much of her sister's very smart words. Forced to face too many things she'd been ignoring. Yes, hoping something would come along to force her into a decision.

How utterly ridiculous for a woman who'd once fancied herself strong enough to run away from a powerful monarchy, hide away on a polar island, plan to raise her babies alone. She, who had whined about having no agency, no choice, was now…cowering in a castle? *Waiting.*

Hiding away from a man who said he loved her? Who wanted to *marry* her and raise their children, putting the children first. Not letting monarchies have any say.

Honestly, it was the most foolish thing, she could scarcely believe she'd fallen so far. Not quite sure what she was going to do about it, she marched out of her room and went in search of Cristhian.

She was shocked to find him not far away, in a room across the hall. Inside the room was…baby furniture. Two cribs. A bureau. She recognized all of it, because they were all she'd bookmarked on her phone.

He glanced up at her in the entry.

"I hope you don't mind me taking the liberty. I thought it best we have the furniture at the very least. Beau assured me you would like these items."

Leave it to Beau. "You're quite right," Zia managed though her throat had gone tight.

"I have some mock-ups of designs for decor. Apparently these things are meant to have themes. You can choose one or come up with your own." He walked over to her, held out his phone.

On the screen was a picture of a beautifully done nursery. It was football themed. She swiped through the pictures from there. Every design offered things they had discussed before. Colors and subjects she knew she'd told him she liked.

Because he listened. Because, and maybe she did not fully understand *why*, he must love her. None of this was the act of a man who did not care.

She knew she had feelings for him, but she'd been trying to keep them…safe. Controllable. Because loving someone, trusting someone, had always been so… transactional with her parents. With friends. And she knew she had nothing special to offer Cristhian.

Beau was the only relationship she'd ever had that felt real, and she'd chalked that up to being twins. And maybe, if she was going to be really honest with herself, she'd even turned that into a transaction. Her protecting Beau in order to earn her love.

No, she supposed it didn't take Psychology 101.

"I think I should like to get married," she said.

He stood very still, his eyes even narrowing a bit as he studied her. "Why?"

She wanted to laugh. It was, somehow, the perfect response.

"Cristhian… My whole life I only wanted someone to care about me…as a person. The way you have shown that to our children has always impressed me, but it isn't just that. You… You have taken *my* feelings into account. As though they matter."

"Of course they do."

"You say that as if you didn't spend the first part of our time here demanding what I should do."

"I suppose that's fair." He sighed, took the phone back and shoved it into his pocket before turning to face her. "And they do matter to me, Zia. They always will. I am not perfect. I suppose I have made and will make mistakes, but I will always fix them. Always."

And she knew that he would. Or at least try to. She had compared him to her father when she'd been angry at him, but her father's orders had never come from a place of care. They came from a place of wanting power.

That had never been Cristhian's way. Even when he'd been controlling, it had been…to make things right. A world safe for their family. In a strange way, it was not all that different from the way she'd acted to protect Beau. Because at the end of the day, she and Cristhian wanted the same things.

The same things.

"How about today?"

"Get married? Today?"

She nodded. "I don't want fanfare. I don't want… anything but us. Promising each other. Because that will be all that matters. As we raise these children together, much will change. But we will believe in our promises, and I think that will make everything okay."

He studied her for another moment. "Zia, I want to get married. I love you, but I want you to be certain. To be sure. I will marry you, if that's what you want, but there should be love. I have always trusted my grandparents' advice. And they have always said love is the foundation. We do not need to start with a ceremony. We can—"

"We started the second I laid eyes on you, and something inside me clicked…as if I knew. As if you were made exactly for me. And I have run from a lot in my life, but that certainty was the most confronting and frightening thing of all. Because I couldn't protect myself on it, or martyr myself to it. And so I have spent all these months trying to convince myself I am not worthy of it."

"Zia. You are beyond worthy."

She didn't know if she fully believed that just yet, but she had faith she would. Just as she had faith now that what she felt, what she had felt all along, was exactly this.

"I love you, Cristhian." And more than the past few days of wondering, she felt so certain now. Because he'd cataloged what he loved about her, and she could so easily do the same. "Your…heart. The way you take care. Even when you are being overbearing and ridiculously heavy-handed, it is only because you are trying to do what is right, and I know too well how hard that can be. Now we can try to do right, together. Maybe leaning on each other will make it less hard."

His mouth curved, and his smile was just like it had been at the bar that night. Charming, special, *for her.*

"I shall call the minister at once."

EPILOGUE

THEY WERE, IN FACT, married that day, with only staff members for an audience, and Cristhian's grandparents and Beau on a video call. The twins were born two weeks later, healthy and perfect.

They named their son after the best man Cristhian had ever known. The newly minted Harrison Sterling would be told of his namesake, but encouraged to live his own, best life. They named their daughter after the woman who had helped set them free. Begonia Sterling, Bee to her loved ones, to avoid confusion.

When Bee met her aunt and namesake for the first time, it was obvious the two would be lifelong friends. And that the Sterlings were in for it.

And when the twins were old enough, they all flew to America, to the same house Cristhian's grandparents had lived in since he'd been born. He was able to introduce his wife and children to the people who had given him everything, in a house he'd once visited with his own parents.

Grandma Connie, as she now insisted upon being called, cried as she held each little bundle. Pop couldn't stop marveling at their size, making sure to read to them every night of their visit.

Grandma Connie even let Zia help with dinner preparation. A great honor indeed.

"It is such a lovely home you have," Zia said, as she worked side by side in the small kitchen with his grandmother. She was beautiful and elegant always, a princess through and through. But she looked exactly right in his grandmother's kitchen.

He'd known she would.

"You grew up in a castle, dear," Grandmother said with a gentle scolding. "I'm sure this is nothing compared to that."

"A castle, yes. Not a home. I didn't have a home before Cristhian, before the children. And now I do, and much of that, I can tell, is thanks to you."

If his grandparents hadn't been willing to love her because he did before that, they certainly did now.

Both Zia and his grandmother looked over at where he sat helping his grandfather with a puzzle. And Cristhian knew that for the rest of his life, only the day Zia had married him and the birth of his children would hold a candle to this very moment in this place that meant so much to him.

Because the foundation of everything had started right here. With love. A love that he now got to pass down.

* * * * *

Did you fall head over heels for
His Hidden Royal Heirs?
*Then you're sure to adore the next installment in
the Rebel Princesses duet,
coming soon.*

*And while you wait,
why not dive into these other
Lorraine Hall stories?*
A Son Hidden from the Sicilian
The Forbidden Princess He Craves
Playing the Sicilian's Game of Revenge
A Diamond for His Defiant Cinderella
Italian's Stolen Wife
Available now!